WHEN LOVE HEALS THE HEART

VANESSA MCKAY

ONE

The guard led Meg to the activity room. The room had polished, concrete floors and a few posters reminding the inmates of prison rules and regulations. *Do not raise your voice, stay calm, go home sooner*, and other similar infographics that you would not come across in normal life on the outside.

'You are our third yoga teacher this year. How did they con you into taking on the job?' asked the guard.

'Money. The money to come here is more than I get for a week of teaching outside, and no overheads,' said Meg.

'You haven't done a prison job before then?' the guard asked.

'First time. I did the onsite training last week; it should be okay. I hope.'

'It will be, we are always here, just don't let them see that you are nervous. They will treat you worse than a substitute teacher in a state school on the last day of term. Don't let on that this is your first prison gig. Tell them you taught at Hakea and Wandoo Prisons.'

'Thank you, I will.' Meg said.

Meg sorted through the yoga equipment left in the room for her: there were mats, blocks, and straps, all looking to be in good condition and coloured the standard uniform orange. A role of inmates had been added to a clipboard on the only table in the room. She picked it up and read through the names. One name stood out. A name she remembers hearing on the news, Scott Clarke. She could see his photo as it appeared in the newspapers a few years back, and she remembered that hewas hot at the time. She smiled to herself; *this just got interesting*.

'You will need to check the role off every time. We need to call their names and hear their voice before acknowledging that they are here, it's the rules,' said the guard.

'Okay, no worries, I can do that.' Meg said.

'Good, look smart, here they come.' The guard gestured to the single line of men appearing at the door.

Meg swallowed hard and took several sips of peppermint water from her drink bottle. She watched the men as they walked in—they eyed her up and down shamelessly, taking in her curvaceous figure outlined in her black yoga pants and racerback Namaste tank top. The simple fact that Meg needed this job strengthened her resolve to stand her ground and not show any weakness. As she saw it, she had two choices, stand tall and proud and stare right back at them, or watch the ground and let them see that she was intimidated by them. She chose to look back at them, one by one, as they passed her, collected their yoga mats, blocks, and straps, and took their designated spots on the floor.

When the last prisoner was seated on their mat, she read the first name from the list. The men stood up, said present and sat back down. This happened with all the men. Scott Clarke took a little longer to follow suit. He was recovering from a broken spine, she would later find out when reading his medical file. The report described the incident as a one sided prison fight.

He was good looking, dark hair and defined features. Even with a broken nose he looked good. A little sad, Meg thought he was still handsome all the same.

When the roll was done, Meg introduced herself, proceeded to have the class stand and adopt a mountain pose, and off they went following her lead through sun salutations as she instructed them through one pose after another. She suggested they could find a way of doing these in their cells between classes. A few nodded their heads in agreement; one said he would give it a try because he always felt less like hurting people after practising yoga.

For meditation she chose a tense-and-release-for-sleep routine. She usually finished each class with a dash of reiki to each participant while they were in silent, rested meditation, and she did the same here. The only difference was that a guard followed her within reaching distance, and she never got close enough to touch the recipient's foreheads when delivering the reiki.

Meg gently drew the class out of their meditation. Two of the men had to be shaken awake by the guard, both coming alive with the fists activated and ready to fight, both swiftly apologising for waking in such a start. Meg assured them that it was a compliment to her class, wished them well and meant it when she said that she was looking forward to seeing them next week.

The men were ordered to pack up and each in their turn returned the orange yoga mat, orange blocks, and orange straps to the portable shelf used to store their yoga equipment. Scott Clarke was the last to leave and smiled at her before wishing her *namaste* with prayer hands and a wink.

She was left alone to gather her things while the prison officers escorted the prisoners to the cafeteria. Meg saw a notice on the board for pen-pals, where prisoners could sign up and be matched with members of the public who wanted to be involved to write letters to help prisoners rehabilitate, to help them feel like worthy members of society. It was a church-run project located close to Meg's house. She wondered how she could be directly linked to Scott Clarke?

The guard returned. 'That went better than we expected, you did really well at keeping them engaged.'

'Thank you,' said Meg. 'Sometimes I guess they just want to act normal, feel like they can be part of something again. This pen-pal thing, is this the only way a prisoner can receive a letter, through a program?' she asked.

'Why, are you thinking of signing up?' the guard asked.

'Me? I have enough on my plate, just curious. But can a prisoner get on with believing in themselves if they are isolated and ignored by the general population? Surely it just takes some understanding,' said Meg.

'Anyone can write to a prisoner, just address it with their name to this address, or whatever prison. I'd wonder why a regular person would want to engage with these guys.'

'Why not? They are here to pay for their crimes and to be rehabilitated, aren't they?' Meg asked.

'I should have known you would be one of those,' said the guard.

'One of what?' asked Meg.

'A snowflake. Let's get you out of here before you start buddying up with the prisoners.'

Driving home through the streets of Kwinana. Megs mind searched for details of Scott Clarke. The name was familiar; his look was intoxicating, and those eyes of his took her breath away. Surely, he didn't do anything that bad, she thought.

Ralph the rottweiler greeted her at the door. She scratched his ears and gave him a treat then ran a shower. *Scott Clarke*, the name was rolling around in her mind like a riddle. She wrapped her long, blonde hair in a towel, dressed in flannelette pyjamas, personalised designer ones with Ralph's face all over them. Now sitting at her computer, she scoured the internet into the early hours of the next morning for everything she could find on Scott Clarke.

Satisfied, that she really was crazy, lonely, and in need of therapy, she fed the patient dog, climbed into bed, and checked in on her Tinder profile.

It was hard being thirty-two and single. Hard to find a decent man her own age that wasn't divorced with kids, that looked after himself, that didn't just want to be with her because they thought that her being a yoga teacher was shorthand for *Kama Sutra* expert.

Meg poured a glass of wine and settled back onto her bed. Ralph jumped up alongside her and after a few belly rubs was softly snoring.

She opened her laptop and looked up Casuarina prison, scouring pictures of the prison for a sight of the inmate Scott Clarke. Meg didn't really understand what it was about bad boys that got her all excited. She had seen the news reports of the crimes of Scott Clarke and still, when she thought of him now, she wanted him. She wondered what she could do to make his life better. Then she saw the menu for prison mail. Pulled an envelope from her desk drawer and addressed it to Scott Clarke, Casuarina Prison.

Meg wondered out loud, 'How do you start a letter to a criminal you can't get out of your mind?'

Dear Scott, I have to tell you that I am a fan of your work...

Dear Scott, I saw you in class today and wondered if you promise not to kill me could we be friends? No!

Dear Scott, thank you for attending my class today. I hope you enjoyed it, and if you wish I could provide you with some therapeutic exercises to help strengthen and repair your back. I couldn't help but notice you had difficulty with certain postures today. No doubt from you recent spinal injury.

I guess, maybe I should tell you about myself. I am thirty -two years old and live alone with my rotti, Ralph. I have been teaching yoga for ten years and have also studied therapeutic yoga for injury rehabilitation. I have worked extensively with senior citizens and generally run a class where I can.

I believe you are a photographer. Does Casuarina run any programs on the visual arts? Can you draw or paint? I am rambling now. Basically, I am writing this to you because there is something I could do to make your time better. I think helping you to improve your mobility will help.

Of course, tell me to mind my own business and I will. But if you would like some help, I will include a few diagram postures here that you will be safe in pursuing until our class next week. Then we can look at how you are doing, and I can provide you with some extra help like this if you wish. The prison won't allow me to see inmates individually on site, but we can converse this way if you like?

Let me know if you would like to continue, Namaste, Meg.

The next day Meg and Ralph took the letter addressed to *Scott Clarke care of Casuarina Prison* to the local post office and sent it on its way.

So just like that, Meg had entered the world of the inmates. She had invited him into her life. She was ignoring the reports and newspaper gossip that depicted the man with dark hair and vivid blue eyes as a monster. Meg focused instead on a wounded man in need of her help. It wasn't ideal, but it was a project that she needed to take her mind off the last year, the miscarriage and the messy breakup that followed.

She felt brave, reckless, and finally free. Meg liked the idea of having a project, and she liked the idea that maybe she could do something useful and worthwhile, like helping to reform a criminal. Why not? She had nothing else planned for the rest of her life.

TWO

During the last five years in prison, he had been beaten, hung upside down in the showers overnight, gang raped, framed for a shanking, barely avoided his own shanking, and held his own in more than one prison fight. Things were starting to quiet down.

He followed Allison's career over those years, despising and loving her even more. He hated that she swelled feelings within him that he was not ever used to. He didn't really like other people. He wasn't what we would call a people person; he liked to watch people from behind the lens of his camera. In prison he watched them over the brim of his law book. The killing and torture of both random strangers and those sad innocents that would class him as a friend had come all too easy to him. He missed the killing, the warm ooze of blood, and the wide-eyed fear of his victims when he introduced them to their own mortality.

He was determined during every beating and torturous assault he received in prison not to give the perpetrators the satisfaction they seeked. Instead, he would stare right into their eyes and question if that was all they had. *Amateurs, all of them,* he thought. He had played with his victims like a cat with a mouse, winding them up, getting off on their fear until he was bored and had to put an end to them.

But that Allison. Her smiling face peered out from the walls of his cell to mock him. How easily she had escaped the punishment he had planned for her. Allison Songbird! He spat the name from his lips like a bug that had crawled in with his dinner. He wanted so much to exact revenge. It wouldn't be easy from a prison cell. They stopped him writing to her, and she blocked his calls and changed her number long ago. He was sentenced for life; how was he going to get back at her? The best he could do was watch. From here he could see the rise of Allison Jones, Songbird. In time he predicted he would see her fall.

Scott called her name through the night just before he slept, sure that she can hear him, that somehow though the graces of time and space she could still hear his voice whispering her name. That he could ruin her dreams with the memory of the things that he did to her. He couldn't let it go. Even with one hundred and more sessions with the prison chaplain, he could not forgive her and set her free.

'But until you stop you are the prisoner, chained to Allison,' the chaplain had said. 'You must let her go.'

'No, I won't. Until my last breath leaves my body, I will think about nothing and no one other than Allison Jones. She ruined my life, her and that stupid fly-boy boyfriend she left me for,' he had said.

After a while, the chaplain stopped seeing Clarke. He was required to report to the parole board on a monthly basis on the progress he was making with the inmates. He was a trained psychologist as well as a chaplain, and the day came that he had to admit that Scott Clarke was a lost cause. He obsessed continually over his one surviving victim and he should never be released, his life sentence should be that, for life. Never before in his twenty-three years of prison work had he made such a proclamation. It cost him many sleepless nights and prayer in consultation with his saviour. Eventually he had to concede that Scott Clarke was filled with too much evil to be saved. There were other, more viable souls that needed his assistance inside the prison walls, and that was where he turned his attentions to.

For Scott Clarke, library duty replaced his visits to the chaplain, and he was taken off laundry duty as a violent risk; there was little one could do with a book, according to the prison warden. Scott used his library time to read all the law books that lined the shelves. Some do-gooders had donated a collection of law books to the prison library when it was built in 1991. Prisoners, they had said, should have access to the law, even when they had been let down by it; innocent people have the right to defend themselves. Scott Clarke wasn't innocent, he was looking for a loophole, one that would lead him back to Allison.

Mail call arrived after lunch. He rarely received anything, just some *Reader's Digest* or free trial magazine he would sign up for. When the officer passed him a hand-written letter through the bars of his cell, he was pleasantly surprised. More so to discover that it was from Meg, the yoga teacher. He was not planning on going back to yoga; it seemed to cause him more pain than it soothed, but after reading and re-reading her letter, he imagined her writing it there in her yoga pants, thinking of him, even giving him extra work to do. She liked him, even cared about him. He was excited at the prospect of having a friend and was prepared to do yoga to get one.

Scott cleared a space on the floor of his cell and went

through the poses that Meg had drawn for him. Cat and dog, legs up the wall became legs up the bars, twists, and hip lifts. He continued to work his way through the exercises every morning, afternoon, and night, sometimes twice a night, and added in some poses that he remembered from class. When Friday rolled around again, he was first in line for yoga class.

THREE

Allison had made it. She stood off stage on the set of the evening television show *The Project*, ready to be interviewed about her new album, *Allison Songbird*. Her palms were sweating. This was the first interview she had about the album, the first ever that didn't involve Scott Clarke. Her agent had given the panel strict instructions that he was not to be mentioned. Allison made this album on her own merits—it was her own music and her own voice; none of this had anything to do with Scott Clarke.

After the interview, she met Robert in the green room. 'You were amazing, darling,' he said as she walked through the door.

'Thank you, I was so nervous.'

'Well, it didn't show. Dinner?'

'Yes, please.'

Out on the city streets, they hailed a taxi and made their way to Darling Harbour on the city's waterfront. They were seated outside on a warm January night and took in the views of the Sydney skyline.

'This is so beautiful,' said Allison.

'You know, I have been thinking that we could move here, away from Perth and close to where your singing, and television opportunities are,' said Robert.

'Really?' Asked Allison.

'Yes, why not? I am often away for work and can always fly to where you are. It doesn't make sense that you have to keep flying across country for interviews, album promotions, and concerts,' said Robert.

'It never occurred to me to move,' said Allison.

'It is just a suggestion; we have no family in Western Australia. I think we should do what is best for us. We will still have our holiday home in Albany to go home to and escape anytime we need to,' said Robert.

'It would be exciting to live here, convenient too. If you are sure, that you are okay with it, let's do it,' said Allison.

The next few months moved quickly. The house they lived in on the banks of Perth's Swan River sold within days of going to market. The house was packed in a week, and Allison flew to Sydney to secure them an apartment overlooking Sydney Harbour. Come April, they were moved in and settled. The complex had a gym, a pool, and several shops and restaurants downstairs that she soon became familiar with while waiting for Robert to return from his latest air force mission.

Allison sang every Friday and Saturday night to packed venues around the city, and occasionally she was a headliner at the casino shows. Everything was going their way: she was writing new music and planning on returning to the studio in September with a new line up of musicians. Musically she was getting a name for herself. She wanted to be with Robert. She wanted him to leave the air force and come home for good, but he still had twelve months on his time to serve, and while they had talked about him coming home to stay for good, nothing was ever really decided. Allison knew that he was torn. He didn't know what he could do outside the air force other than re-enlist as a reserve agent. He had promised to look into private contracts, but so far there were no positions that would allow him to be home for the long haul.

Allison would like him to stay, yes, but her own work that was so very different from his would require her to travel too. How could she clip his wings and not expect the same to be done to hers? She was due to go on tour in November and then again in the following year and so on for as long as her career demanded it. And when she was honest, she knew that she wanted to take it as far as she could for as long as she was able to. It was all she ever wanted, something that she had been told in the past she could never achieve, and now here she was a singer, with fame and enough money to buy an apartment overlooking the Sydney Harbour Bridge. It was easy for her to be happy now. Everything was coming up roses.

FOUR

For yoga day at the prison, she dressed in a white kurta top, long sleeved and uniformly modest, over leggings. She had been told in the briefing not to wear anything too revealing, she didn't want the prisoners getting the wrong idea. She was there to help them, and that was what she intended to do. Especially the prisoner Scott Clarke. He had entered her dreams this last week. It served no rhyme or reason other than the fact that maybe she had been alone for too long.

Driving her little, yellow Suzuki Swift to the prison, she thought of him; unpacking and repacking her bag at security, she thought of him; while being searched by Trisha, the only female on staff at Casuarina that had to work every yoga day, she thought of him.

Meg lit the incense sticks in the Buddha holder that she brought and handed the lighter back to the guard. She scanned her notes and worked on keeping her breath calm to dispel the butterflies. She would be seeing him soon. What if he thought that she was a nutter, that there was something not wired correctly with a yoga teacher that would at first glance send an inmate such a letter. *Let's be friends, I can help you feel better.* Her brow beaded with sweat, she suddenly felt a fool.

The men began to come into the room in single file, most making eye contact with her, some daring to greet her politely. The inmates had been warned at the commencement of yoga classes that the slightest inference of inappropriate behaviour would see them in the hole for an unspecified period of time. The rules were clear. All privileges were based on good, upstanding behaviour. Any deviance from that path would be dealt with harshly.

Taking a deep breath, she busied herself with her notes as the men were settling in. When Scott entered the room he smiled broadly at her. The class went without incident; she was able to manoeuvre around the room and offer verbal adjustment queues where required. The men on the mats were keen to follow her instructions, and she felt that she was going to able to make a real difference amongst the chosen inmates. At the end of the class, she made the suggestion that the men should be practising some postures on the days when she wasn't there, to help speed up their progress and further allow the benefits of yoga to seep into their everyday living. Scott raised his hand and told the class that he had been practising some of the postures and found them most beneficial. She understood his meaning, smiled and suggested that he keep up the good work. This caused the group to move into the conversation of which poses would be more beneficial, and together as a class they were able to devise a small routine they could all practice. Four postures to do in rotation, the beginning of the Sun Salutation.

When the inmates were packed up and leaving the room, Scott was the last to leave.

'Thank you, Meg, for the exercises you gave me. I really appreciate you thinking about me,' said Scott.

'You are welcome. I am glad that they helped you,' said Meg.

'Move it along, Clarke,' called the guard.

Meg exhaled deeply when she was finally alone in the room. He had thanked her, and she felt exhilarated. He was good looking, and his voice was deep and resonant. *What are you doing?* she asked herself again. *This is madness.*

Meg followed the guard out the prison building and through to the exit gates. Looking back at the prison, she felt sadness that anyone would be locked in there, particularly her Scott. He was not the man that they spoke of in the newspapers, she was convinced of it. He didn't have the eyes of a killer, a monster, like the man they said that he was.

When she arrived home, a letter waited for her amongst the electricity and phone bill and credit card statements. It was from him. Prisoner 3227, Casuarina Prison. Her heart leaped and beat hard within her chest.

She unlocked her door and was greeted by Ralph. She let him kiss her face, and he wagged his tail like a whip against the wall in high-speed thuds. Meg gave him a treat, which he scoffed in seconds, and took him out the back of her fibro-cement home to relieve himself. She watched from the porch as he sniffed the same trees and poles he always did, peed on the same spots he always peed, and finally circled an imaginary spot before taking a poop.

'It's all right, boy, I have got your back, I will look out for you.'

He glanced over and completed his task, wiping his paws on the grass when he was done.

Meg scratched his big, boofy head, kissed the soft, velvet

of his muzzle and followed him back inside. She put on the kettle and made herself a cup of tea. The letter was still in her hand; she glanced at her name on the front of the envelope. She sat on her bed, and Ralph jumped up to join her. She rubbed his long, black, soft belly. 'I think I might have gotten myself into something I am not sure I know what to do with. How could I be lonely when I have you. No. This is just work. I am excited about having a job after all this time. A steady income is nice. No more turning up to empty studio classes, boy. Yes, that is all it is. He is a customer, a student that I am being paid to help, nothing more.'

Meg took a sip of tea and was soothed by the warm camomile and honey taste. She took a deep breath and opened the envelope.

> *Dear Meg,*
>
> *Thank you so much for thinking of me. I really appreciate that you took time out of your life to send me those diagrams and postures. I do think they are already helping me. I practice every morning and night now. I have a cell to myself, so there is no problem with me practising in here.*
>
> *Can I ask you a question? I have trouble when I do the forward bends in the sun salutation, even with the blocks. My back injury prevents me from reaching the floor. Can you suggest something that can help me there?*
>
> *The blokes on the block were ribbing us last week about doing yoga, but now they see a group of us practising in our cells I think that they are a little pissed that they didn't sign up for it themselves. Bigger fools them, I say, and maybe more work for you in the future.*

I hope that you do not mind that I am writing to you. It is hard to talk to you during class with so much done in silence. But thank you for coming and teaching yoga, not many women would want to teach us losers, and fewer still would be able to look past the things that are said about me and take a moment to help ease my pain.

Is it okay that we communicate? Don't let the fact that I have no one left on the outside sway you. But you seem like a very special lady, and someone I would like to get to know better. Your friend and yoga student, Scott.

'What do you think, Ralph? Seems harmless enough to me.'

Ralph snored softly at her side. Meg pulled out her notebook and began to write her reply. Later she walked Ralph to the letterbox and dropped the letter through the slot. *And so begins my relationship with Scott Clarke the serial killer, it will be fine, he just needs a friend, that's all.*

That night alone in her bed she re-read the letter he wrote. She smelled the paper trying to get a scent of him and reads his words again. Turning out the lights, she listened to the soft snoring of Ralph by her side. She replayed the day's class, focusing on Scott as if he were in a spotlight and there was no one else there. Just her and Scott. The sound of her own voice moving him through the postures and him obeying every word. Doing her bidding. In her replay he was fluid and strong; she left out the weakened, bent spine, the broken nose and hands. The Scott she saw was the man from the newspapers, the handsome serial killer. It could never be the same man. She thought of him being found innocent, his imprisonment as some miscarriage of justice, and he would be free. She would pick him up from the gates of the prison. He would kiss her passionately like in the movies; it would be slow motion, and romantic music would rise up from nowhere. They would drive away in a yellow convertible into the sunset to begin their lives together.

In the dark she rolls her own eyes. Her imagination often ran away with her, and make up scenarios in her head. As a child she was always creating new realities out of sucky situations. Meg knew that there was nothing that could go on between her and this man, Scott Clarke. She sat up in bed and fumbled for her laptop, opened it up and Googled his name. The first articles to appear where those about Allison Jones; apparently, she accused him of stalking her, raping her, kidnaping her, and attempted murder. He was described as a jilted lover. The articles featured photos of her with some guy in an air force uniform with his arms around poor little Allison. Meg took stock of her reaction. Was she jealous? Of whom? Allison?

Meg kept digging through the older articles, the ones of his crimes and the things that he had done to people. The homeless man he murdered, the couple, the woman and her son in Albany, the doctor whose head he smashed, and all the other evidence that mounted up against him. Amongst the online history she found his Facebook profile, unused for many years. There she saw pictures of a Scott Clarke she wanted to get to know. She was indifferent to the descriptions of him in the tabloids that described him as a monster, someone that should never be released from prison again. Facebook showed her something else. A man she would like to get to know. There were travel pictures and well wishes from friends and memes and gentle ribbing like you get with your friends online. *Where were these people now?* she wondered. How quickly everyone can disappear when your life turns to shit. Where were the pictures of his friends standing next to him in the courthouse? He seemed to be all alone now, unwanted and regarded as an evil monster. Once he was considered an attractive, outgoing man, adventurous and well liked. Meg wondered what had happened to him to make him turn. Was it stress? Was he possessed? Was it that he was just innocent?

Closing the laptop and returning it her side table, Meg lay back on her bed. Staring into the darkness with her hand resting on Ralph's flank, she wondered what was the harm in communicating with Scott. Maybe he did do all those things, and if so then he would be forever imprisoned for his crimes; if he didn't, then one day he could be re-trialled and released and maybe he could use a friend on the outside to help repay him for the crimes inflicted on him by an unjust society. So as far as Meg could see, there was no harm in being nice.

FIVE

A letter arrived two days after class. He opened it in the quiet of his cell.

Dear Scott,

Thank you for your letter. I am glad that you found the exercises that I gave you useful, a regular practice will improve your range motion, so I am glad to hear that you and the other men are practising in my absence.

Regarding your reach problem, I have enclosed a diagram with breathing exercises that will help you open up your chest and bring blood to your muscles.

Let me know how you get on. I am always happy to help, and yes, I would like to write to you. It is nice getting to know you. We really do not have enough time during class to get to know each other.

I would like to know some more about you. Simple things like, where did you grow up? What did you like to eat when you were a child, you know what was your favourite meal? Please don't say

McDonald's. I mean something you were excited to sit down at the dinner table for. That was made just for you.

I know it may sound like an odd question. I had a pen pal growing up. She was from Germany and we would always ask each other a question about our everyday lives. I am hoping that maybe this is something we could do, to get to know each other better and to better understand who we are. I am afraid that you will think me crazy, but I have enjoyed receiving your letter, and it is such a pleasant and some would say old-fashioned thing to do, I would love to continue.

Namaste,

Meg

Scott laid back on his bunk. He stared at the photos staring back at him. Allison, there coming out of the courthouse, looking smug with that Robert by her side, his arm around her. His eyes rested on Robert's knuckles, and he rubbed his jawbone where those knuckles had crushed his teeth on the that day in Williams. She must be something to have caused so much trouble. If it weren't for Robert, he would have gotten away with killing Allison, he was sure of it. He could have kept her out there in Albany, in the forgotten forest. No one would have found them.

Another photo, their wedding, so precious: the bride in white lace, the groom in tails with a flower in his lapel. So proud he must have been. So hot that wedding night must have been. Turns out he did her a favour, the attention she received from the capture—the newspaper articles, the news stories, the 60 *Minutes* exposé. The *Woman's Day* and *New Idea* articles all helped to move her career forward. Look at her now. She was a star; she made it, she had become everything that she wanted. Allison Songbird was a star, a singer, and a recording artist. And he helped her becomes who she was. Without him she would be a singer on cruise ships or downtown karaoke bars.

He held the letter to his chest. *Meg,* he said the name out loud. Meg wanted to know about him, about who he was. What he had for dinner? An odd question, but he guessed she was a nice person and would not want to know about the bad things that he done. She wanted to know about him, about the nice things. It had been a long time since anyone asked him about the normal things. People these days just wanted to know about the why of it, what happened to make him act like a monster, why did he hate women, men, people. Why he didn't let that boy in Albany go, what was his relationship with Deborah, whoever she was. Meg, this could be the beginning of a new era. A friend. No one in prison talked to him, no one asked how he was feeling, no one cared.

He could hear Meg's voice in his ears. He sat on the edge of his bed and pulled a pen and writing pad off his side table.

Dear Meg,

Thank you for your letter. It makes my day to see your letter in the mail. I really appreciate you taking the time to help me. The new exercise you gave me is helping. I never would have thought of doing yoga before. I wonder what made you decide to teach in a men's prison. I am so glad that you did. Without you I would not have any friends on the outside.

About my favourite thing to eat. It is a loaded question that takes me back. I remember coming home from school and smelling the roasted chicken. My mother would make the best roast chicken meal you ever had. Roasted potatoes, turnip, carrots, and cauliflower with cheese sauce. It was the gravy that made it. Oh, and the stuffing too, sage and onion from the garden. Breadcrumbs from the leftover bread that she made herself, the chicken from the coup. I grew up on a farm, in country Victoria, with Mum, my grandparents, two brothers, and a sister.

I am curious about you. Tell me about your favourite meal, is it from your childhood? Something that somebody made for you. Where did you grow up?

What is it that you think about when you are taking a yoga class, or teaching a yoga class? I am curious about why you became a yoga teacher at all. Were you needing to heal yourself? What type of yoga are you teaching us? No one asks you any real questions in class. I wonder if they are afraid of you.

I look forward to seeing you again on Friday and receiving your next letter, it really means the world to me. I feel happy, like I have a connection with you. Sorry, I hope that doesn't sound too weird. I don't want you to get the wrong idea. I know we could not be anything more than pen friends, it is just so cool that you are mine. (I sound like a teenager.)

It is nearly lights out, so I will say goodnight. Take care and sleep tight, my yoga guru. Your friend, Scott.

He folded the letter, placed it in the envelope, and addressed it carefully. He put his prison-allocated stamp on the corner and put it on the side table, ready to give the designated postie the letter to send in the morning.

He smiled at the thought of Meg, somewhere tonight lying in her own bed. What if she wasn't alone? He didn't want to think of her with another man—or woman, for that matter. She had mentioned a dog. Ralph. A rottweiler. Tomorrow, he would look them up in the library. He knew what they looked like, but he wanted to be able to talk to her about him and sound like he knew what he was saying. He wanted to impress her, and it was hard to from his position, lame and in prison.

He got up from his bunk, and in the small space next to it he went through the movements of Sun Salutation, making the adjustments that she recommended. He closed his eyes and repeated each side three times. When he was done and opened his eyes the cell was dark; it took a moment for his eyes to adjust and see the outline of his cell. The bed, the toilet bowl coming out of the wall, the small side table, the desk along the wall. He sat on the floor, in easy, cross-legged pose, and inhaled deeply. The stale air in his cell was different from the incense-scented air when Meg was here. How could he get hold of some incense, he wondered. *No mind,* he scolded himself, *just breath, focus on your breath, inhale one, two, three; exhale one, two, three.* He could feel himself calming, his shoulders dropping down. When a thought passed his mind he breathed, one, two, three.

When his block was settled in and quiet, he got into his bunk. The face of Allison was drowned out by the sight of Meg. Allison was the past, Meg was now, and now was all that he had. This was prison. He was never to be paroled, and any day someone would take a hit out on him, just to prove that they were worse than he was. His reputation coming into prison was one of a cold, hard, calculating serial killer. He was predatory, he was calculated and cold yes, he had planned everything down to the final detail. Even his attack on Ally that night of the party his things had already been packed; he already had a place to go and hide away from the cops. It was true he might have gotten a little carried away. She did anger him so, so smug and perfect. The doctor, that was admittedly off the cuff.

Maybe he did have a violent temper like the psychiatrists said, perhaps he was a Jekyll and Hyde. He didn't know. As far as he knew, he had never changed.

He wondered what would have happened if he had met Meg outside, before all the prison chases and stalking and killing. What could they have been?

He could have walked into a yoga studio, probably somewhere like Fremantle, and sign up for a beginner's class to help him with that back pain that sometimes niggled him. She would have been there, her long, blonde hair over her shoulders, wearing those yoga pants and a crop top, because she wasn't in a prison studio. They would have talked about the things they liked to do, movies they had seen, what they liked to eat. *Maybe we could eat somewhere together*, he would ask—no, not right away but eventually, he would have asked her something. *Hey, how are you doing? What do you like? Do you like me?* He could take the mat front and centre because he wouldn't be ashamed about his broken body, his body would be okay. Not beaten and broken in untold places like the wreck he was now. How a few, short years have changed him. He could have become her best student, rolled up her mats and carried her equipment to the car. He could have followed her everywhere and done every class that she taught. Maybe he could have become a teacher. Maybe they could have gone on retreats together. He could take her photos in all sorts of scenery: Bali, India, Japan, Singapore, the forest, the bush, the city. He could see her in all of those scenes. Beautiful, exotic, and contemporary.

He held her letter to his lips and kissed the envelope, inhaled it, but already it stunk of the stale, prison air. Her name was the last word to pass her lips before he slept that night.

SIX

Allison woke with Robert lying behind her, spooning her, his arm tight around her waist. He nuzzled in the space between her shoulder blades and breathed in her scent.

'Good morning, lover. I really must ask you to leave; my husband will be here to make mad, passionate love to me any second now, and he won't like an audience,' said Allison.

'I have already changed the locks. That husband is no good for you leaving you alone and wanting,' said Robert.

Ally spun in his arms and cast a leg over his hips. 'Robert, I am so glad that you are here. I have missed you so much,' said Allison.

'Me too.' He kissed her softly.

She moaned and explored his familiar mouth with her tongue; tightening her leg she pulled their groins together.

They were fumbling now to remove each other's underwear. She was wet and ready to take his hardness.

He turned them both so that he was on top and entered her.

She arched her back and called his name. 'Robert.'

He tried not to rush, but he had not been here for three months. It had been too long; he missed her and the feelings she gave him. He slowed his pace to line the nape of her smooth neck with kisses; he felt her skin become goose-fleshed.

She giggled and ran her hands the length of his body, and when each hand came to rest on his taut butt cheeks, she thrusted her hips into him, pulling him deeper in to her.

He couldn't hold back; his pace quickened. He saw it in her face that she was on the edge, about to come. The wait had been too long for them both. Her nails were digging into the flesh of his buttocks. Helpless now to do anything but go with her pace, he followed her on the crescendo of her orgasm, releasing his own at her peak. They hung on tightly to each other, her legs wrapped around his tanned, taut, muscular body.

'I love you, Allison,' he said.

'I am so glad your home. Would you like some breakfast? I have been shopping.'

'I know, and I already have everything ready, so rest here, my love, and I will be back with your breakfast.'

Allison watched as he got up from their bed and stretched his towelling robe around his frame, smoothing down the fabric when it was tied, and walked out of the room. *He is delicious*, she thought.

Allison lay in the bed and closed her eyes. She listened to the sound of him singing in the kitchen, the clatter of cups and plates being arranged, the whiz of the juicer. She thought she should get up and go and help him, but he did say that she should stay here. Besides, she wanted to make love to him again, slowly. His absence had been hard on her, she had missed him, and she wanted to show him just how much she loved him, so very much.

In his absence, she went quietly into the bathroom, brushed her teeth, tidied her hair, and generally freshened up. They were not going anywhere today, except back to bed if she had anything to say about it. She jumped back into bed and smoothed the covers just as he entered the room carrying a tray of croissants and the fresh fruits, she had bought for him, fresh brewed coffee and the juice she heard being made.

'You spoil me,' she said, kissing his cheek.

'I have to, you are the most beautiful woman I have any known, and that I get to be married to you is amazing, which is why I also have tickets tonight, courtside no less, to see the Wild Cats play the Sydney Kings,' said Robert.

'Tonight?' Allison asked.

'Yes, unless you had other plans. Please say you don't. I have not seen a game in such a long time, and I really want to go with you, my hot, sexy, lady—we can go out for dinner afterwards, make a night of it. Then tomorrow, I will bring you more sweet treats in the morning, and then because it is Sunday we can take the ferry over to Bondi, body surf, market, and drink beer on the grass of that little beer garden we found on the corner.'

'You mean, Clancy's Cart?'

'Yes, that one. What do you think?'

'Sounds wonderful. I did have something else planned, but perhaps we will be able to fit some more of that in after breakfast.'

Later that day she awoke from a post love making nap to hear the bath in their ensuite running. Soft music played, and she smelled the scented candles burning. Walking into bathroom expecting to see a bath prepared for her, she was pleasantly surprised to find Robert surrounded with bubbles, eyes closed, his head resting on her bath pillow.

Allison smiled, discarded the chemise she was wearing, and climbed gently into the bath. He smiled when he felt the water shift, opening his eyes to see her lower herself between his feet.

She smiled, turned, and lowered herself to lie on his chest. They lay there together until the water began to turn cold. He soothed her hair and held her securely in the water while she listened to the soft, rhythmic beating of his heart with her ear on his chest.

Reluctantly Allison lifted herself off his body, left the bath and ran the shower. She turned and smiled at him, and he soon followed up on the invitation.

That evening they sat court side while the Perth Cats played the Sydney Kings, premium seats meant that they attracted the attention of the local media, and it did not take long for them to work out that she was Allison Songbird out on the town with her handsome husband. During the breaks at quarter times the cameras stopped on them, prompting them to act. In one shot she kissed Robert on the cheek, and he feigned embarrassment. Another time Robert stood up, got down on one knee and re-proposed, another he stood up, had Ally do the same, and swept her up in a passionate, romantic kiss. The pair's antics were all over Twitter before they left the stadium.

From the game Robert and Ally caught an Uber and went to Nine Dragons in Chinatown. They ate their favourite dumplings with plum sauce, vegetarian fried rice, and shared a fried ice cream for dessert.

'Let's go dancing, Robert,' said Allison.

'Now, with Chinese belly?' said Robert.

'Yes, why not, we are talking about having a family, and

as lovely as that sounds it will change our whole way of life. Let's be spontaneous while we can,' said Allison.

'Did I mention you look beautiful tonight?' asked Robert.

'Yes, but I still want to go dancing. When I am working all those people get to dance to the music that I make. Sometimes I want to dance too, with you, and let someone else make the music while we make our memories.'

'How can I say no to you. You are right, smart, and super amazing,' said Robert.

'I think you are a little drunk,' said Ally.

'No more than you, my love. I think that we should go dancing.'

The waiter, Bao, recommended a club near Darling Harbour and ordered the pair a taxi. Soon they were on the dance floor. The disco lights swirled, fellow dancers boogied in faux cages, and the crowd on the floor pulsated to the rhythm that the band was pumping out. The crowd pushed Allison and Robert closer together, holding onto to each other, their hips swaying in time to the music.

'This place is amazing,' said Allison.

'I am glad that you talked me into coming here. I love seeing you dance, and I love dancing with you,' said Robert.

The band played a slow song, the last number for the night. Allison and Robert held each other; she rested her head in the space between his chest and the curve of his neck, breathed in the scent of him. She felt his arm tighten around her waist and lifted her head up to kiss his mouth. A soft, slow lingering kiss that continued until the song had finished.

'Let's go home, Robert,' said Allison.

The chill from the early morning Sydney air was sobering. No cabs or Ubers were answering their calls, so they began the walk home, stopping occasionally to kiss and to check Robert's phone for a taxi or Uber. Giving up for the time being, Robert entered their home address in Google Maps to make sure that they were taking the right way home.

The air and city were almost still. When they rounded the bend that led them underneath the Sydney Harbour Bridge, the monument towering above them in the dim, early-dawn light, they heard a group coming down the ramp off the bridge entry. A group of young men, dressed alike in black hoodies, pipeline jeans, and desert boots. They passed without incident; still Robert held a protective arm around Allison and made eye contact with the boy in front.

'Just lads out for the night,' said Allison.

'I know, but you can never be too—"

Thud. Robert was knocked in the back of his head. He doubled over as Allison called his name. 'Robert, are you okay?'

He held the back of his head, took his hand away to look, and it was covered in blood.

'Ally,' he said.

She was trying to hold him, as he fell to the ground. She screamed for help, looking around. There was no one anywhere, just the dark, cold, morning light creeping over the harbour.

Ally called an ambulance. Using the location on Google Maps, she was able to tell the operator where they were. A voice on the other end kept her talking while she sent an ambulance and a police detail to their location.

Ally was questioned briefly by the police and told that this gang were known to them, and it was not the first time that they had attacked an innocent person out of the blue. The officer that questioned her wished Robert a speedy recovery and told her that he liked her music as he ushered her into the back of the ambulance to travel with Robert to Sydney General Hospital.

She registered little other than the in and out breaths that Robert made. The ambulance officer patched up the wound and was trying to talk to her and to Robert. She held his hand and willed him to squeeze her, *Anything, Robert. Please*, she said silently.

'A moment ago, we were dancing in the club, then they knocked the life right out of him. How? Why would they do such a thing...'

The ambulance officer looked at her across Robert's body. 'I know this must be very hard for you, but there is no reason that this happened, it is just a stupid, dangerous act. It had nothing to you, with who you are. They went off and are probably home tucked up in their beds thinking nothing of you or of Robert, no consequence. They think they are above the law. We are called to so many violent attacks on innocent people, and there is just no reason satisfactory enough and no punishment a deterrent enough to stop people being arseholes.'

'But he is all that I have. I can't lose him,' said Allison.

'We are doing everything that we can to bring him back to you, Allison.'

'We are going to start a family. We just moved here from Perth for my career, and he is taking steps to leave the air force so that we can spend more time together. He cannot leave me now. Please tell me that he is going to be okay!'

'We are doing everything that we can. They will be able to tell you more about his condition at the hospital. I will be praying for you both.'

SEVEN

Meg scruffed Ralph's head as she walked in the door, and he followed her to the treat jar.

'You have trained me well, boy,' she said, passing him a strip of chicken jerky. He gobbled it up in seconds and followed her to the back door. Meg moved the sprinkler along her vegetable patch and turned on the tap. She sat on the step and watched Ralph sniff his rounds around their back garden. She could hear the neighbour's children playing in the yard and inhaled the tapestry of dinners being cooked near open windows in the houses that surrounded hers.

Ralph came to sit beside her. Meg ran her hands along the length of his black coat; his breathing slowed, and he closed his eyes.

'How was your day, boy?' She took a drink from the bottle of pear cider she picked up on her way through the house. 'It was tough today. Mum didn't know me today. She kept calling me Rachael. Her sister was called Rachael. You remember her, she always saved the lamb roast bones for you from family dinners. She loved you. I miss her too. I bet you are missing the lamb bones more. The nurses say that I do not have to go and visit her every day, if I had better things to do, but honestly, where else could I be? What could be better than looking after my own mother after everything that she did for me? I wonder if she is in the right place. Maybe I should look into some other homes. What do you think, boy?'

Ralph snored softly at her side. She sat with him, gently rubbing his torso until he woke himself up with a fart.

'Come on, boy, let's go for a walk,' said Meg.

Ralph wagged his tail and followed her through the house, sitting patiently at the door waiting to be dressed in his fine collar and lead. Meg locked the door behind them, and together they headed to the park. She followed him as he led her from tree to tree, waiting for him to explore before moving on. It annoyed her to see people pulling their dogs along by the leash, hurrying their pet's one big adventure for the day. She firmly stood by the belief that dogs may only be a part of our lives, but we are their whole lives and she intended to make Ralph's great. The first time she saw him was in the adoption shelter. She had gone to foster an abandoned little rottweiler puppy that was not coping well with being in the shelter—not that any dogs do. She fell in love with him instantly, and apart from work and taking care of her mother she spent all her time giving him the world. In return he adored her, protected her, and made her feel safe.

That night in bed with a wine in her hand, Ralph at her side, she opened the letter saved until now to open. She knew that it was from Scott, but she had wanted to wind down from her time at the nursing home, the fight she had with the bank, and the small misunderstanding she had with the yoga studio manager that insisted that they didn't have space for 'her kind of yoga'. They had just enlisted the services of a Bikram instructor and that was the hottest thing out right now, even with all the allegations directed at Bikram Choudhury.

Meg needed more work. The prison was working, and it was enough to carry her through from week to week, but if she was going to move her mother, then it would not be enough.

'Sure, and sitting in bed at eight o'clock every night obsessing over a prisoner will help?'

Ralph raised his head to look at her, exhaled, and returned to his dreams.

She opened the letter. It was not going to hurt. She read the letter out loud quietly to herself. Ralph snored softly through the recitation. She folded the letter and returned it to her envelope, smiling with herself. Getting up to pour herself another glass of wine, she flicked through the channels on the television, glanced over at the letter, and turned the set off. Read the letter again, fetched another glass of wine, a pen and pad of paper, and returned to her bed.

Dear Scott,

I am so very glad that you are finding yoga useful and that you are seeing some improvement in your mobility. To be honest, I was having a hard time finding work, so many yoga classes now are controlled by flashy, overpriced studios. It is just too hard to break through the noise, hiring halls, and pinning notices to cork boards. The job at the prison was advertised through an agency and I took a chance, passed the clearance test; and the rest, as they say, is history. The job takes a lot of pressure away from me in trying to find customers. I am consid-

ering setting up a private studio at home and practising yoga therapy on a one-on-one basis, just sorting out the process now.

I like your story of your mum's roast chicken dinner. Living on a farm is so different from growing up in the suburbs. My mum use to make lasagne, layer upon layer of delicious, roasted vegetables, zucchini, pumpkin, tomatoes, steamed spinach leaves, and red sauce and cheese sauce, between layers of homemade pasta. It was such a treat. There was just mum and me, and it would take us a week to eat. We didn't have farm, but mum grew all her own vegetables. I look after her vegetable garden now.

When I am teaching a yoga class, I watch how my students are moving. I need to make sure that I am giving you all the correct verbal cues. You may sometimes hear me say the same thing a few times in different ways, because not everyone understands the way I say things the first time. They each have their own way of learning and understanding. Taking class is no different inside than on the outside, the motivation for me is the same, I want to help you all feel better. That is not exactly true—I mean, yes, I want to make you all feel better, and for you to take away some tools that you can use between classes. The other differences are that I cannot touch you, according to the warden anyway, and I need to arrive an hour before each class to get inside. They pay me so I shouldn't complain. It would be nice to have another class like yours, to be honest. It is very forward thinking of your warden. It would be nice to see more of it, *not just for my benefit of course. I think everyone should yoga.*

I became a yoga teacher when my mum was first diagnosed with MS to help her, and myself, because it is hereditary. So just in case, it will be helpful either way to keep my body healthy as I age. It is a nice thing to do, teach yoga, practise yoga too, but you are already learning all about that yourself. I just wish I could reach out and do more.

I really enjoy reading your letters too. Yes, pen pals is a childhood thing, but there is absolutely nothing wrong with that.

Please keep writing, I look forward to seeing you Friday.

Namaste. Your friend, Meg.

Meg folded the paper and addressed the envelope, sealed it, addressed it to Scott Clarke care of Casuarina Prison. 'Do you think that I am crazy, boy?' She rubbed Ralph's flank, and he sniffed her hand in search of a treat.

She got up and he followed her into the kitchen, refilled her glass and poured another glass. Meg put the empty bottle in the recycle bin, where it clinked against the others. She stood at the back door waiting for Ralph to finish his late-night constitutional around the garden. She scruffed his head as he entered; he waited as she locked the door and padded behind her back to the bedroom.

Lying in bed, Meg flicked through the channels on the television. She watched the late news and saw Donald Trump refusing to surrender the White House and the new president had a German shepherd. Not much else of importance. She flicked around the channels again and settled on a re-run of *Friends*. It reminded her of the time when she was with Charlie. Watching Friday night *Friends* was their thing: Domino's pizza and sitcoms. It was the perfect way to end the week, to let go of stress, to dream of something else.

She picked her mobile phone up from the bedroom table. *Hey, Charlie, want to hang out, may be a Friday session with reruns, wine, and pizza? Luv, Meg.* She hit send. Returned the phone to the table, closed her eyes, and with heart racing she took a deep breath.

The phone buzzed in reply. *Yes,* it read, *that would be awesome see you Friday xx.*

She lay back on her pillow, smiled to herself. It had been so long since she had company other than Ralph. She scrolled through Facebook on her phone. There was Charlie beaming from the pages surrounded by people Meg did not know. How had they grown so far apart? she wondered. She hit the thumbs up to like the photos and continued to scroll. Charlie had a wine and confetti profile; Meg's own was a bland, few pictures of herself and her mum and a few of Ralph. Compared to Charlie and her other yoga friends, it looked pathetic. Her Facebook page was just like her life—pathetic. She would have to ask Charlie for help on Friday.

EIGHT

Robert was taken to surgery to repair a bleed on his brain while Allison was ushered into the small waiting room designed by the architects to house families waiting for bad news. Ally made herself a cup of tea to wet her dry mouth and pass some time. The tea was grey and tasted like overnight sink water, but she drank it down. It was her fault that they ended up here. Robert hated to dance, he only went for her, and now he was fighting for his life. All anyone would tell her was that they were doing the best they could. She was afraid that they were setting her up for bad news.

Her own face stared out to her from the magazine on the table. There was an article about her move to Sydney and how she and Robert had plans to settle here and start a family.

She took out her phone but realised that she has no one to call. She was all alone without Robert. She scanned her list of contacts. She could call her agent, but then she thought twice, knowing that if the press got hold of this story it would become a circus. She texted Amber in Perth.

Don't answer me if you just woke up but call me in the morning. xx

The television droned in the background and blended with the noise outside the door. She felt forgotten. Allison rested her head back on the seat. What if they had forgotten all about her, what if Robert was out of surgery and everything was okay and so happy that they just forgot all about her? Nerves danced in her stomach. She checked her phone; it was only seven am. Allison poked her head out of the door. She saw the nurses gathered in behind the desk exchanging notes for change over between shifts. She watched and waited, trying to remember the nurse that had told her to stay here so many hours ago.

As she returned to the vinyl couch, her phone beeped.

Hey Allison, how are things going over there is everything alright? We are looking forward to coming to see you next month.

Allison wasn't sure about what to say.

She would explain later. She didn't know what was happening, how Robert was, and she was sure that she couldn't begin explaining it without breaking down, and right now it was taking all she had to hold herself together.

When the nurse came in and told her that the doctor would be with her in a moment, she felt relieved, but then panic kicked in. What if it wasn't good news?

When the doctor came in, he looked exhausted. He explained to Allison that the hit and subsequent fall had caused a crack in Robert's skull and pressured a vessel in his head that ruptured and bled. They were able to stop the bleed, top up his blood and repair his skull with a plate, but they were not sure what damaged had been done nor how it would affect him. He was just in recovery. Once he was moved to the intensive care unit, she would be able to see him. The doctor went on to explain that Robert would be kept in an induced coma for the next seventy-two hours to ensure his best chance of recovery. He encouraged her to go home, have a shower, a rest and return later, promising that Robert would be in good hands until she returned.

'Please, doctor, I just want to see him first, if that's okay?' she asked.

'Of course. I will have a nurse take you through when he is out of recovery. It may take an hour or two. Maybe try get some rest here. I could have someone bring you some breakfast, decent coffee at least?' he offered.

'Thank you, doctor, that is kind of you, but I really just want the chance to see my husband, please,' said Ally.

'I understand,' said the doctor. He left her alone.

Allison closed her eyes and focused on her own breath entering and leaving her body. She thought of Robert in his hospital bed; healing, resting, out of danger, needing her, and, mostly, she knew, her needing him. She clenched and unclenched her sweaty palms and remembered his face, his sweet, beautiful, downy face.

'Sorry to keep you waiting,' a voice interrupted her. 'Would you like to see your husband now?'

'Yes, of course,' said Allison. She gathered her jacket and purse and followed the nurse out into the hospital hive towards Robert.

'Here you go, just a few minutes for the time being, let him hear your voice. And then on doctor's orders you should pop home and get some rest, a shower, and bring back some clothes and sleepwear and such to help you both be more comfortable. We will set up a cot for you if you want to stay the night.'

'Thank you yes please, I want to stay,' said Ally.

She took hold of Robert's hand and squeezed it with no

response. His head was bandaged and there were tubes coming from his head, another going into his nose, a tube was breathing for him. He wore a hospital gown, the sheets pulled up to his chest. He was the pale, like they washed the sun and the life away from him. 'Robert.' She choked on his name.

Nurses came and went, busied themselves around his bed and generally avoided eye contact with Allison. When one was still long enough, Ally said, 'I will pop home to grab some things; will he be okay?'

'Yes, he will, he is just resting, go and get yourself sorted. We will take good care of him for you,' said the nurse.

'Thank you,' said Allison, letting go of his limp hand and leaving the room.

The Uber drive that collected her from the hospital recognised Allison right away. 'You are that singer, Allison, aren't you,' he said.

'Allison, yes,' she replied.

'Allison Songbird, in my car,' he said, 'wait until the wife hears about this one. You think we could have a picture?' He leaned over to the passenger side of the car and snapped his phone before she had a chance to register what he was doing. 'I will send that to the missus when I have dropped you off. She will be so happy—well, not really, she will be jealous,' he laughed. On and on he bantered about all assumptions he had about what it must be like to be her, how lucky she was with all the overnight success, all that fame and money. He wanted to play guitar apparently, and he could have been really good if he ever had the time to practise. His voiced droned in her ears for the next fifteen minutes. She did her best to not encourage him to continue or to be rude. Smiling in the correct places, nodding her head here, shaking it there. Allison was barely holding herself together, but it wasn't his fault, he had no idea what she was going through. Relieved to be outside the doors of her building, she exhaled as he beeped his horn in farewell and drove away.

Ally stepped into their apartment and slid down the inside of the door, collapsing in a heap of tears and snot on their floor. Her heart was breaking. *He will be all right*, she said to herself over and over again.

She smelt his pillow and held it close to her, remembered the day they spent together yesterday that seemed so far away from where she was now. He will be all right, *where attention goes energy flows*, she remembered her yoga teacher saying in class, *focus on good, manifest good*. Robert would be home, and they would be making love on these sheets again soon. He would be holding her in his arms, kissing her, loving her, and everything would be all right.

She showered and packed their things in a case, called a taxi. Uber drivers were always so chatty, chasing good reviews, normally she didn't mind, but today she needed all her strength and energy for Robert.

Back at the hospital Allison collected some magazines and mints from the gift shop and headed back to his room. A foldout bed had been set up in his private room as promised. He was in the intensive care unit, a glass wall looked directly into the nurse's station.

Staff came in every half an hour to check his vitals. A menu for meals was sent up from the kitchen, and the young girl who delivered her afternoon tea shyly admitted that she was a fan of Allison. Most of the staff here knew who she was, and her staying here was the talk of the lunchroom.

'So sorry for what happened to your husband. They will take very good care of him here,' said the girl.

'Please don't tell anyone away from the hospital that I am here. I don't want to be creating trouble with press stalking us here. I don't have the energy.'

'Well, they certainly won't be hearing about it from me. I will tell the others to keep tight-lipped too. No worries from the hospital staff. They are not allowed to discuss a patient's personal details outside the work area. Privacy laws and all.'

But it was too late. A nurse's aide had texted her friend that worked in Myers and told her she had just seen Allison Songbird. She was overheard telling another sales assistant by a junior editor at *New Idea* magazine, and she immediately texted her boss the news, hoping to get brownie points at the office. A reporter and a photographer were dispatched to Sydney General, and that alerted *Woman's Day* spies, and so it went on, that by five o'clock that afternoon the biggest story in town was that Allison Songbird's husband was admitted to hospital in a critical condition and all shows were cancelled so that she could be by his side.

It didn't matter that she hadn't even had any shows booked for the next six months because she was due to head into the recording studio. It didn't matter what happened, it took days for someone to find a snitch at the police department to tell them what happened. Truth didn't matter. Somehow, they managed to get a photo of her at Robert's bedside, and then the picture from the Uber driver turned up in the papers. The vultures had swooped in, and it was the price of fame that she didn't expect, and she was quickly regretting her choices. All she wanted to do was to sing and live her life with Robert.

NINE

S cott woke in his cell. He could hear the summer rain outside, and he raised his head up to the dank ceiling of his prison cell. The other inmates were still sleeping. He could hear their faint snoring and nightmare renditions humming through the walls of the cell block. Sounds of misery. Mostly.

He stood slowly, relieved himself in the pot, washed his hands, and rolled out his bath towel on the cement floor of his cell. Standing at one end he inhaled, exhaled, cleared his mind of his surroundings and thought of Meg, in front of his tiny room. He heard her voice instructing him, *On your next inhalation raise your arms up to the sky....* Without her, he let her take him through the sun salutations; he honoured Mother Earth and Father Sky, the makers of all things, as he inhaled and exhaled breath throughout his body. He started to feel many things, new and old things returning with these practises, from obscure pieces of himself to the most obvious. Firstly, which was startling to a casual observer being that his mobility was improving, he was starting to feel again, become human, he thought. So much of the last few years following his arrest he had been treated like a monster. An animal. A soulless man. He had been prodded and probed by medical doctors, psychologists, and to what end? To declare that he was fit to stand trial. Was he? What if there was something wrong with him that was out of his control? No one knew, no one really asked, no one cared.

Here the doctors did enough to shut him up. Pethidine when he had to spend nights in the infirmary. Panadol when he was sent back to his cell. No one had really looked at him in the last five years, without disgust, fear, or morbid wonder.

Scott bent forward, inhaling, lifting up slightly and exhaling to reach his arms towards Mother Earth. He could feel his spine expanding as he reached towards Father Sky and felt the warmth of an absent sun on his face. Meg continued to guide him, and for this time on his makeshift mat there was only her and him in this world.

After a quiet breakfast in the canteen, he attended his assigned duty in the library. Newspapers were delivered today, a few days behind schedule, but when you are on the inside even old news is new. He browsed through the pages of *the West Australian* and saw Allison looking drained and tired. SONGBIRD'S HUSBAND HIT WITH COWARD'S PUNCH, in critical condition. Scott rubbed his jaw and let his hand follow the bumps of scar tissue Robert left with him that day, the teeth he shattered, unrepaired beyond simple efficiency. *How perfect*, he thought, *her life is falling down around her ears again*. He smiled; the news coupled with Meg and his newfound love of yoga lightened his step.

When he had done his rounds with the library trolley he returned to *the West Australian* and tore out her picture, folded it, and slipped it into his pocket. The rest of the paper was left in the recreation room along with *The Times* and puzzle magazines.

That afternoon he found a book in the library about Bikram Yoga and devoured the pages. He took notes. Wrote out questions that he thought to ask Meg. All this time he felt he had gone unnoticed, but she saw him. She could see past the man he used to be to the man he was now trying to be. He stopped then to ask himself, what kind of man did he think he was? Or could be? Was he always so tied up with being obsessed with how other people saw him? Did it matter? Would that really change him?

This Bikram Yoga character didn't help him much. He was prancing around in his underwear, touching women and pushing them deeper into poses with his own body. There had to be something better. This didn't seem like the kind of yoga Meg was teaching, but it was the only book in the prison library on the subject. He did speak briefly of having a guru and that your teacher should be a guru, a person you believed you could follow on your journey. Was Meg a guru? What was her guru training? Would she be his? Could he ask? Is that what he wanted? Suddenly he felt anxious. He was used to being a despised monster, but this needy git he was playing didn't sit right with him. He had to be stronger, but wanting Meg was weakening him.

Scott put the yoga book back on the shelf and placed an order on the inter-prison library order page. There were benefits to not working well with others; most days he had the library to himself. He liked being alone, but only when he chose to be, which was most of the time. He set about returning books to the shelves, his last task for the day. His thoughts jumped from Meg to Allison. Why did he feel so differently about the two women? Allison, he wanted to possess, to lord his power over her, to use her. To see her in pain gave him pleasure—even thinking of it now still warmed him, made the blood rush through his system, lifted the hairs on the back of his neck and tented his trousers. If he could, he would kill her this time, he knew it. She did not deserve to live, he just wouldn't be able to say why. Other than it pleased him. Was this a god complex? He pondered. Meg was different. She was attractive from the right angle; she had a nice, soft, rounded, yoga body that was pleasing, and he was sure more than one of the blokes used the image of her posing on her mat to help them get some relief at night. He didn't. It cheapened her, and he didn't think that she should be cheapened in that way. Meg was more than a woman, more than someone that he wanted to use and manipulate, she was something else entirely.

Meg's letter arrived on Thursday. He had panicked all day on Wednesday that she didn't want to have anything to with him. That night he had drawn pictures of Allison, the way he had posed her for the photographs, and in ways he would have should he ever have the opportunity to so again. He had taught himself to draw inside. It was a small compensation for his loss of photography. No lens except his memory now, he could shadow, brighten, and manipulate the images he put on paper.

He left the canteen now holding the letter to his chest and closed his cell door behind him. He sniffed the envelope, looking for a sign of her. It only smelt of paper and the grubby hands that processed it. He pulled his cell table close to his bunk, sat down, opened the envelope and removed the paper. Fold by fold he straightened it until Meg's letter was laid flat on his table. He took in the paper. It had changed, this was writing paper, not copy paper the other letters had been written on. This letter had a delicate picture of a lotus flower on the top, proper writing paper. He smiled to himself.

Reading the letter, he tried to picture her writing. He had her sitting at a white desk in a yoga studio, mat rolled out, buddha in the corner, her hair swept up, mala beads, a candle burning, all the yoga cliches` were used to build the picture in his mind.

When he was ready to reply, in his mind's eye he changed the surroundings he was in. He was sitting on green grass, next to a lake, a soft breeze playing in his hair, and the walls of his cell disappeared, Mother Earth beneath him and Father Sky above....

Dear Meg,

A joy, such joy to receive your letter. I have been practising twice a day now and have a couple of questions that came up from the only yoga book we have in the library to read. But I will get to that later.

I thank the agency that brought you here to teach us yoga. I am sorry that you had a hard time finding regular work before you came here, and you know I hope that you will keep coming for a long time to come.

The lasagne your mum makes sound amazing, home grown vegetables too! I bet it was delicious. I don't mind admitting that you had my mouth salivating as you described the layers. The cook here does something he has incorrectly called a lasagne. It is just meat and a layer of pasta with a smidge of cheese on top. I wouldn't like to think what kind of meat it is. Where is your mother now, do you see her often? Are you still close? My mother died a while back. We weren't close, we just were.

You must be so busy running your own business and taking care of Ralph. Thank you for taking the time, I wonder are you writing to other inmates too? It's just that I don't want you to be doing too much, that's all. Does that sound awful, like I am saying don't write to other prisoners? It is just that maybe don't write so often. I love getting your letters, but I do not want to be a nuisance. You are so kind with your time. I don't know that I am saying this right, but please do not stop writing to me.

My days here are very routine, particularly now the other inmates have lost interest in beating me up, tying me up, stealing my stuff from my cell, tipping over my tray, and pushing me around in the showers. I work in the library most days. I am on my own. It is my job to push a trolley of books around to the other cells and deliver books to the prisoners. You would be surprised with what some people read in here, we have requests for everything from Jane Austen to Stephen King and, yes, Shawshank Redemption is a big one! Today I read a book about a yogi named Bikram. Can you tell me what you think? My first impression is that life is hard enough without doing yoga in ridiculous temperatures, and in the photos where he is teaching, he seems to enjoy taking liberties with the lady students over the men. He looks an old perv to me. Sorry if you are one of his students, I do not mean to be insulting. I am sorry again...as if saying sorry immediately cancels out something nasty that I might have said. I always hate people that do that.

I am off track. Can you tell me what your take is on Bikram and his style. Also, tell me something you do when you are not working. It doesn't have to be personal, just something about your life beyond the wall; it would be nice to know what you get up to.

I can start. I wake up at five every morning, lay my towel on the floor and do sun salutations, as best as I can, remembering your words and what you told us about Father Sky and Mother Earth. I imagine that I am between them with no concrete between us. Once the prison begins to stir, our cells are opened at seven. We shower and have breakfast, then I go to the library and sort the delivery for the day. After lunch I do my rounds with the trolley then back to the library to put the books away. Dinner, reading, bed. That is all. Not very exciting, which is why I am sure you will understand that your world is so interesting to me.

Namaste

Your faithful student, Scott.

TEN

Meg put down the tray of nibbles and poured the wine.

'So, Meg, tell me, what have you been up to since I last saw you?' said Charlie.

'Well exciting news. I have a job, full time with excellent pay. I am my own boss and I literally get to do what I want,' said Meg.

'Well, that does sound exciting! Where is it, who is it for, and what is it worth?'

'Nosey little fucker, aren't you? Well, it is for the department of corrections. I am teaching at Casuarina Prison, the men's prison. Once a week, and for that I get enough money to live off for the week!' She smiled.

'The prison, Meg, are you mad?' said Charlie.

'No, I was desperate and tired of turning up to empty halls. God, I was even trying to get a job pushing trolleys at Coles, so when this came up, I thought, what the hell, I am safe, there are guards with me all the time.'

'If you are sure, it is safe, well then I am happy for you,

and sorry, I had no idea things had gotten so bad,' said Charlie.

'What about you? What have you been up to?' asked Meg, refilling her wine glass.

'Well, I was supposed to go and do backing vocals in Sydney with Allison Songbird, for her new album, but something happened to her husband, and she had to cancel,' said Charlie.

'What! Allison Songbird! That is amazing, you are in the big time now!' said Allison.

'No, I was nearly in the big time, maybe, I don't know,' said Charlie.

'Look, the fact that you got the job, that you were all set and chosen to be there, means that you have been noticed. Like I always told you, Charlie, you are a star! Here, let's drink to your success.'

'I know, but apart from back-up work in the studio, I haven't been on stage with any of these big names, I am just beginning to doubt that my time will ever come,' said Charlie.

'I know what you mean. Look at my life,' said Meg.

'I am sorry, I shouldn't complain, most of my life I have been able to work towards the things that I wanted to do, while you worked here with your mum,' said Charlie.

'It's okay,' said Meg.

'How is the job going, is it scary?' asked Charlie.

'It was the first day, I really didn't know what to do, but I was told the prisoners were warned that any muck around and they would be off the program, no exceptions. They don't talk too much, mainly hello and thank you at the end of class. It is hard to read most of them. I think I am going to try to get them to open up during class, talk to me more, so at least I will know that I am doing the right thing,' said Meg.

'Be careful, you are not turning into one of those women that fall in love with a man on death row,' said Charlie.

'You idiot, there is no death row in Australia,' said Meg.

'You know what I mean, you deserve a real relationship with a man that treats you like a goddess,' said Charlie.

'I don't think such a creature exists,' said Meg.

'I'll drink to that,' said Charlie. 'Hey, why don't we dress up and go out like we used to? Go on, put something sparkly on and lend me something hot that you are too afraid to wear.' 'I don't know, what about Ralph?' said Meg.

'Dress him up too. As long as he doesn't cramp my style, we will be sweet,' said Charlie.

Getting out of the Uber at the front of the Sunset Hotel, Meg and Charlie were arm in arm striding towards the front bar when a familiar voice stopped Meg in her tracks.

'Meg?'

'Andrew, what are you doing here?' asked Meg.

'It is my stag night. I am getting married. I came home to get married,' said Andrew.

'Getting married?' asked Meg.

'Yes, to Rachael, we met at work. I am sorry, I wanted to come and see you, tell you in person, but I just couldn't bring myself to do it. After all that you have been through,' Andrew said.

'You mean after all that *we* have been through?' said Meg.

'Yes,' said Andrew.

'It is okay. Congratulations, Andrew, I hope you and Rachael have a wonderful life together. I truly wish you all the best, and I am glad to know that you are happy and have moved on with your life,' said Meg.

'Thank you. What about you, are you seeing anyone?' asked Andrew.

'I am, as a matter of fact, his name is Scott. We met in one of my yoga classes. He is not the usual type of man I would fall for; he is tall and very handsome, so please don't feel bad for me. We are having a great time. I am just out with Charlie tonight because she was stood down from her gig with Allison Songbird, she had to cancel her recording gig when her husband got injured,' said Meg.

'Well then, that is great. It is so good to see you and tell you my news and hear your great news too.' He held his arms wide for a farewell hug.

She obliged and said nothing, just nodded as he bid her goodbye.

'Well, you deserve a fucking Oscar for holding your shit together.' Charlie put her arm around Meg, hailed a taxi, and ten short minutes later they were back at Meg's house.

Meg gave Ralph a treat, ruffed his fur up, and finished the glass of wine Charlie had just poured her.

'He is getting fucking married. To a slut no doubt, to a twenty-nothing-year-old fertile, normal-family-related, fit slut!' said Meg.

'She could be fat,' offered Charlie.

'No way, did you see how fit he was looking? She is younger and she is fit, there is no other explanation for it,' said Meg.

'He could be dying of an incurable disease,' Charlie offered.

'No,' Meg hiccupped, 'he has moved on. He is not looking back, he has no need or want or care for the life that we use to have, the one we shared.' Meg bawled.

'He wasn't good enough for you, Meg, he was never good enough for you. You always deserved better than he gave you, and after all that you went through, he left. Just when your life could not be any tougher, he bailed on you. What an utter prick. And besides, you have this Scott man you neglected to tell me about before,' said Charlie.

'Scott? Scott, I do not have any man and certainly not Scott. I panicked. I didn't want him to think that I was alone and pathetic, I wanted to him to think that I had someone better too.' She blew her nose into a tissue and dropped it behind the couch. 'Do you know how pathetic I am? I will tell you, because you were there when I stuffed my bra for the blue light disco you were there through all my embarrassing, pathetic moments. "Scott" is Scott Clarke, the man that tried to kill your future boss, Allison Songbird. He is in my yoga class at the joint. He is serving life for being a psycho, and he is the best made up boyfriend I could make up!' Meg filled another tissue with snot, dumped it and drunk down the wine that Charlie gave her.

'Scott Clarke...he is handsome, I remember him from the papers. But, Meg, you really aren't involved with him, are you? I mean, there is still a chance of finding love on the outside, a normal man that will treat you good. Please don't tell me that you have fallen for a killer and rapist. There is bound to be someone better than that on Tinder. Come on, let's look.' Charlie pulled out her phone.

'No, Charlie, I don't want to look. I miss him. I miss Andrew; I miss our life together. Every day I think of him, and all this time I thought maybe while he was working out there in the Artic, he was thinking about me too, but it turns out he wasn't. I can no longer pretend that he will one day knock on that door, take me in his arms, kiss me romantically and you know there would be music and fireworks—and we would live happily ever after. But now I know we won't. I am not involved with Scott Clarke. No one. It is just

Ralph and me, and I visit my mum every day after she has her breakfast. This is my lot in life and working at the prison doesn't only help to pay my bills but reminds me that my life could be worse,' said Meg.

'Yes, it could. I am so sorry, we should never have gone out,' said Charlie.

'Yes, we should have. If we didn't, I would never have known the truth, and I would waste more precious time dreaming of a love that will never be. Things were never the same after I lost the baby. He doesn't owe me anything. Our life together was just more than he was able to handle.'

'There you go again making excuses for someone else being an arsehole,' said Charlie.

'Charlie, he can't help that his shoulders were not broad enough to carry the burden of who we were together as a couple. To overcome our losses and our troubles. Yes, he is a pissweak little fuck, and I am not denying any of it, he turned away from me when things got hard, at a time when I know I would have dug my heels in deeper to help him. He deserted me. I am not an idiot. I just wish it could have all been different,' said Meg.

'I know, and there is nothing wrong with you thinking that it should be.'

ELEVEN

Day three in the hospital. No one could tell Allison what to expect, they just didn't know. She had been visited by her agent, the hospital chaplain, and a representative from the victims of crime support unit, the police, and the women from the hospital benefit fund. She felt so alone, and as much as she wanted to reach out to Amber, she knew that she was busy, and while she thought Amber was the nearest thing she had to a best friend, the feeling probably wasn't reciprocated. That was fine. They had not known each other for long. Renee was Allison's best friend, and she was sure that Amber had other people too. God, when this was over, she was going to make an effort to reach out and cultivate friendships, it was important, Allison's mind rambled on in circles.

Robert's family were satisfied that he was in good hands, and that there wasn't a need to rush to Sydney to see him. Confirming what she already knew that he was closer to his grandfather than any of his remaining relatives.

There was no solace in writing in her journal. In that hospital bed lay her best friend in the world, and without him everything else was just pointless. A waste of her time and energy. She needed him to wake up! Sitting next to his bed she held his hand and counted the machine taking his breaths.

'Robert, can you hear me? Please wake up. I need you. I have been so caught up in my career, I didn't stop often enough to thank you. My wonderful husband. I am scared, lonely, and want to hear your voice again.'

'How about my voice again?' said Amber at the door.

'Amber, oh my god, I can't believe that you are here. What are you doing here?' Allison leapt up and hugged her. 'I can't believe you are here.' She sobbed, releasing everything that she had been holding in.

Amber held her, smoothed her hair, and let her cry.

'Where else would I be? You are my dearest friend. We have been through so much together, and well, if you like I can stay with you for as long as you need. Woods has everything under control back home. Besides, I was looking into quitting soon.' She leaned back and rubbed her stomach, outlining her rounded belly.

'Oh my god, you are pregnant, how long, oh how wonderful, why didn't you say anything, wow, this is incredible, congratulations! Robert, look, Amber and Woods are having a baby. We were planning on starting a family, well at least stopping trying not to start a family.' The tears came again.

'Well, I am five months today. Sorry I didn't tell you, I wanted to wait until we were on video chat to tell you face to face. Imagine if you fell pregnant soon. Our babies can grow up friends.'

Allison wiped her eyes and blew her nose. 'I will jump on him the minute he wakes up. I just want him back, Amber.'

'I know but wait until I leave the room! Meanwhile, fancy a walk to the cafeteria? You look like you could use some fresh air, and baby is hungry, well, I am hungry, and the baby just justifies my hunger.'

When they arrived back to Robert's room the nurses were moving him from intensive care. They took out his breathing tube and explained to Allison that he would no longer be kept in an induced coma, it was up to him to wake up now. They were positive and upbeat as Amber and Allison followed Robert on his hospital bed being wheeled through the hospital and into a private room on the general ward.

A new cot was brought in for Allison, and she gave Amber the keys and directions to their apartment. 'Go to our place, make yourself at home, and get some rest. I can't believe that you are here, but it truly is so good to see you. But I planned on staying here until Robert is out.'

'Okay, sounds fair enough, any sane person would do the same. I can be your go between home and here. Give me your dirty laundry and directions as to what you would like me to bring in for you. I will work here as your personal assistant, incidentally, why is it that the famous Allison Songbird doesn't already have a personal assistant?'

'I just haven't needed anybody. My life is pretty simple still, so I never thought I needed one. What my agent doesn't do I do; she has a personal assistant, but she is busier than me, I guess. Should I get one, so you don't have to?' asked Allison.

'Don't be ridiculous, I am happy to be here, to help you, and feel useful. Woods won't let me do anything at home, and at work I am constantly assigned to some important admin work while the rest run off to play. No, please let me help you, I want to,' said Amber.

Later that day Amber arrived at Allison and Robert's apartment. It was beautiful with views of the harbour. From their window she could see the Sydney Harbour Bridge and a tip of the Sydney Opera House. She called Woods and gave him the video tour of the apartment.

'How are you feeling, really?' he asked.

'Tired, and, oh my god, take a look at these ankles.' She lowered the camera to reveal her swollen ankles.

'Sit down now, take off your shoes, and put your feet up, please, for the baby, for me,' said Woods.

Amber did as he ordered, sitting on a cream chaise lounge near the window, her feet free for the first time today. She told him of Robert's condition and asked that he look into the case from his end.

'Allison is only just holding it together. I am glad I came; she doesn't have anyone else. It's not fair, all that pain,' said Amber.

'She has you,' Woods said.

'Yes, I would like to be here for as long as I am needed, if that is okay.'

'Of course, just promise me that you will take care of yourself and come home before it is too late to fly in your condition,' said Woods.

'I will, I promise. I love you,' said Amber.

'I love you, go rest,' said Woods.

'It's only five o'clock here,' Amber protested.

'Then go and eat, Rick's at the door with beer and pizza,' said Woods.

'Oh, I see how it is, the second I leave the state it's pizza with the boys. I like pizza,' said Amber.

'Then order yourself two, one for you and one for the baby,' said Woods.

'I will. Goodnight, please don't pine for me,' said Amber.

'I will always pine you, my love, that is why Rick is here to hold my hand while I watch the footy,' said Woods.

'Oh good, you will be all right then, love you. Talk to you tomorrow.'

She hung up and ordered herself a pepperoni and pineapple pizza via the Uber Eats app on her phone.

At the hospital Allison picked through her visitor's dinner. They gave her a vegetarian salad that she would have normally enjoyed, but tonight she had no appetite. She watched Robert's chest expand and deflate and thought of all the wasted moments. The times they didn't get to spend together. She needn't work so hard, he could retire, now, his time in the air force was nearly up. Their time should be now. They should move back to Perth, maybe Albany. They could put an extension on his grandfather's shack; it would be peaceful, quiet, and it would be just them. She could join the Country Women's Association, sing locally, go back to karaoke, anything just to stay near him.

She was holding his hand. She could feel the sweat on his palm and the vibrations before she saw it. His body was seizing. She buzzed for help, called for help. Afraid to leave his side, she kept her hand pressed on the buzzer and yelled, 'HELP! HELP! HELP!'

A nurse stuck her head around the door, about to tell her off for holding the buzzer, but saw Robert and yelled down the corridor for the crash cart. Allison was pushed aside as hospital nurses and doctors surrounded him. His bed was lowered; he was flatlining. It took three shots of the defibrillator, an adrenaline shot to raise a faint pulse. His breathing tubes were replaced.

Allison was allowed back in once most of the staff had cleared the room. Like before she packed their things and followed the bed through the hospital to the intensive care unit.

Allison pulled out her phone then thought twice about calling Amber. There was nothing that she could do; it was ten o'clock and she must have been exhausted. She had travelled all the way from Perth to Sydney. Pregnant. Just to be here for Allison.

She put her phone back in the bag. Pulled up a chair to Robert's bedside and whispered in his ear. 'Robert, what the hell are you playing at? You can't leave me, not like this. We have too much living and life to experience together. Remember me, come back to me, please stay here with me. I know that you can fight this; come back, please.' She sobbed with her head resting on his bed until dry. She slept.

TWELVE

Today was yoga day, and in spite of his worries Scott was looking forward to seeing Meg. He woke early as usual that morning and practised his sun salutations. During breakfast he played with the reconstituted eggs and baked beans, going over the letter he wrote to Meg and trying to work out what it was that he had said that made her not write back. He concluded that it must be because he asked her if she was writing to other inmates. Had he come across as jealous? Did that frighten her, was she finished with writing to him? He was determined that he must get to the bottom of it. Whatever it was, he needed to know.

He was first in line today. She had said hello as he walked in; he nodded, unable to prevent himself from feeling annoyed. He laid out his mat and immediately assumed Tadasana, mountain pose, with his eyes closed as the other inmates found their spots in the room. He worked hard at deepening his shallow breath, but his chest was tight.

Meg's voice instructed the class to begin in mountain pose. 'Draw your kneecaps up, belly button towards your spine, shoulders down and back; chin up and head tall, inhale one, two, three, four; exhale one, two, three, four...' She continued, and he couldn't help but fall under her melodic, soothing, yogic charm.

Scott was into downward dog when she came over to him. He could smell her patchouli perfume before he heard her voice.

'That is very good. Try to activate your belly, draw your naval towards your spine.' She placed one hand on his stomach the other on his spine, drawing his attention to the area.

He instinctively drew his belly away from her hand.

'Sorry I didn't write this week, it's been a busy week.' She released her hands and moved on with the class.

Busy week? he thought. There, that explains it. Whatever has been happening to her on the outside has kept her too busy to be communicating with me. There must be so many more important things to keep a woman busy on the outside. As hard as he tried to be mad at her, he was guided by her voice, his arms and legs moving at her direction. His lungs expanded and deflated at her bidding.

At the end of the class, he rolled up his mat and was first to leave. He didn't want to stay under her spell: she was warm, calming, and dangerous to his survival. He had to stay alert in prison. It was only a matter of time before another round of beatings began. He wasn't sure how many more he would survive. The yoga she brought him was his only pleasure, the only place that he could find peace, but even here with all the *namaste* and goodwill there was still a chance that someone would have a go. It just took one new bloke on the block that was yet to have a go, that hadn't had a shot at the notorious serial killer, maybe to prove something to themselves, maybe to make themselves look like a tough nut in prison, maybe because they really despised woman- and child-killers. He never asked, he didn't really care. He just wanted to survive. He believed that he would be free again one day.

Back in his cell he took out the last letter that Meg had sent him, read word by word, letting each one sink in like a stone in a pool of water, resonating with him, settling in his mind. He told himself that she didn't want to write to him, but a little voice countered with *she was busy*, she thought of him first, he had done nothing wrong to change her mind, they were friends. She had to know that she would always be safe from him, that he did not see her like that, like a victim. To him, Meg was special.

When he was satisfied with the words that she had already given to him, he took out his pen and paper and penned her a letter.

Dear Meg,

It is okay that you could not write to me this week, I understand that your life must be very busy. Unlike mine. I have plenty of free time to think on my faults—that is the whole point of prison, I guess. Thank you for class today. You smelled nice and looked so beautiful. I want you to know that I have a lot of respect for you and truly honour the time you take when you do have the time to send me a letter. I want you to know that it means the world to me. You are the only person in the world on the outside that bothers about me at all, that cares and talks to me like I am still a human being.

In a nutshell, I want you to know that I appreciate you.

Thank you,

Your faithful loyal student, Scott.

Satisfied with his humble apology for ever thinking bad of Meg, he folded the paper three times, placed it in an envelope, addressed it to Meg, took it to mail office, and returned to the library hoping that the library books he had ordered from the central database had arrived.

THIRTEEN

Driving home from prison, Meg thought through the events of the last week. Meeting Andrew wasn't good. Catching up with Charlie had been fun but made her realise that she herself wasn't having any fun, she wasn't really following her passion. If she was honest, she had no idea what her passion was. She took up yoga to help her mum and because it was better than working at the mushroom farm. She liked painting and drawing but felt like she was just wasting time in college. There wasn't a job at the end, not unless you were amazing or wanted to be a teacher, and besides mum had needed help.

Had Scott been weird? He had flinched when she touched him—she wasn't supposed to touch the inmates, but she was a yoga teacher, and it was natural to perform physical adjustments on her students. Meg wondered what it felt like for him. All those years of being inside, no one touching him with kindness. She had Ralph and her mum and friends and yoga classes, lots of well-meaning love and kindness around her. It saddened her to think of him alone without any love. How was he ever going to heal from the darkness that haunted him? It must be a dark, evil presence. It wasn't normal, or even human, the things that he had done to those people. Yet when she thought of him now, she felt pity. He was a lost, broken, battered human being in need of kindness, and, yes, love. Could she show him the healing love of the universe that she had found through yoga? Could he find some peace in the universe and go on to be a better man? Was it possible to do good in the world from behind bars? He could mentor other prisoners, maybe he could learn to be a yoga teacher himself. Teaching in prison helped others see the 'light' like born-again Christians in prison did; why not be a born-again yogi? What if she could develop a program for helping prisoners be better? That could be something that put her yoga on the mat! Meg nodded her head in agreement.

Ralph waited for her at the door. He greeted her with his wiggly bum, and she knelt to hug him while he kissed her. They headed straight to the treat jar; she held him out a choice of three, and he picked his favourite of the moment before retiring to his bed to enjoy it.

The idea of helping prisoners through yoga appealed to her more and more, but where to start? In her office she sat down to Google 'prison yoga programs'. She took notes, the benefits, the risks, and the ultimate outcomes. Scott ran through her mind. His demeanour today wasn't normal. Something was off. She poured another glass of wine for herself and changed her Google search to Scott Clarke.

Meg again found his original Facebook profile. No sign of murdering tendencies here, just a young man in the prime of his life celebrating with friends. She recognised two of his victims in the picture, a couple he allegedly murdered in their own home while he was searching for Allison. It did not make sense. These were his friends as well. There were no pictures of Allison. surely his page would make mention of her somewhere if he had been so obsessed with her.

She printed out his profile picture and made a list of his favourite movies, music, and hobbies. A photographer, a printer, a gym junkie; he was fit, handsome, and cool, he was an 'it' man in his twenties only a short seven years ago, so different from the man she saw in prison.

Meg watched the printer cartridge travel back and forth over the paper, rubbing his image onto the page. His hairline, the forehead, his eyes, line by minuscule line she watched his face appear. Not today's Scott, this was the Scott she would run into at a pub, maybe dance with and kiss at the end of the night. It was hard to place him in the prison and attach him to those crimes.

She poured herself another glass of wine, pinned Scott's picture to the wall. *You better be careful here*, she told herself. *You think he is a nice man, but no one can do the things he has done and be a nice man. Unless they are crazy.* Ralph stirred at the sound of her voice, slunk down from the bed, and nuzzled his broad head under her hand.

'All right, boy, let's get your dinner,' said Meg.

He padded behind her to the kitchen and waited patiently next to his bowl. She filled his dish with chicken mince, kangaroo steak, brown rice, grated carrots, and pumpkin.

'Maybe I am looking at this the wrong way, Ralph. Maybe I need to see what he has done wrong so that I do not get too hung up and taken away by his good looks. What do you think, boy?'

Ralph raised a paw and gave a slight groan in plea for his dinner.

Determined to find the truth, she googled Scott Clarke again with 'arrested' tagged to his name. Crime after crime, accusation after accusation, she listed them all, making note of his victims, what he did to them, whether they were alive or dead along with any other relevant information she could scrounge. She looked up court dates and planned to go to the Supreme court offices on Monday to track down court transcript records.

She poured another glass of wine, let Ralph outside for his constitutional, and watched him as he sniffed around the garden looking for the place to leave his dog rocks. When he was done, he ran inside like a champion having victory over his day.

Sitting back down at the computer, Meg searched for Allison Jones. What was it about this woman that obsessed Scott so? She read interview and after interview, both about Scott and about her career. She printed out a picture of Allison on her wedding day from *New Idea* magazine and pinned it next to Scott. How very different their lives had turned out. What would have happened if these people had never met? Would she have married the lovely Robert? Would Scott be in jail? The picture of Allison smiling back at her with Robert at her side made her wonder why Allison was such bad luck. He was in the hospital now after being attacked in Sydney. Was she the problem?

Meg could find little information about Allison before Scott Clarke entered her life. She appeared several times in Renee's Facebook, but her own Facebook page didn't exist until post Scott, just before her career took off. Was he the reason her career took off? Was Allison Jones, one time bar singer, destined to be a nobody until Scott Clarke made her famous? Did she have Scott to thank?

Meg lay on her bed. Ralph jumped to her side as she rotated the ideas of Scott, Allison, fame and Robert around her mind until finally the wine got the better of her and she found sleep.

FOURTEEN

Allison stirred from her sleep slumped over Robert's bed. She became aware of the hiss and puff of the machine breathing oxygen into his lungs. Then an orderly came in, bid her a good morning, and left a breakfast for her on the tray table. Ally had no appetite. She straightened Robert's hair. His face looked so drawn. She messaged his commander telling him about Robert's condition, the new complications, and the fact that no one here seemed to know what to expect next, never mind if he would make a recovery.

The next visitor brought a newspaper and left it on her tray. She flipped through the pages and saw that the boy responsible for Robert's injury had been charged. Police had told her, but she had not seen the photo, a young boy around seventeen, in a private school suit flanked by his parents. Two lives ruined for such a dumb, cunt act. She took in the image of him and his sad, disappointed parents, she could not help but feel sorry for him. No one sets out to cause such misery, no one except Scott Clarke, she thought, but yes, even he had something wrong with him, there was some glitch that made him do those things, there had to be. It was not human.

The tea lady came, and Ally took a white coffee with one sugar. The hospital was stirring. Ally could hear the busy chatter of hospital nurses and doctors: orderlies transporting patients, bed pans being cleared, medication delivered, breakfast plates shifting. The still, dark night had passed. Robert was still here, and she took a moment to be thankful for that.

Amber woke at ten, felt her baby kicking and rubbed her hands over the expanse of her swelling belly. She smiled to herself, burped, and made a dash for the toilet. Morning sickness had been an on-again-off-again curse for her from the beginning. When she was done, she showered, dressed, and face timed Woods. She smiled through a quick call with her hungover husband, and then was soon on her way back to the hospital.

When she found Ally and Robert had been moved back to the intensive care unit, she was exhausted and feeling a little seedy by the time she found them.

'Are you okay,' asked Allison.

'Yes, just, morning sickness. Why didn't you call me last night, I could have come back,' said Amber.

'Really, you are too much. No, there was nothing that you could do, there is nothing that I can do. We just have to wait. I don't understand why any of this happened, why he won't wake up. I am glad you are here, but don't overdo things. Please you don't have to worry about me. That won't do us any good, it is more than enough that you are here,' said Allison.

'I called Woods today. He is going to touch base with the people involved,' said Amber.

'I already know one has been charged. I am guessing

they will only charge the one that threw the punch. Look at him, here.' She showed Amber the picture in the newspaper. 'He is just a boy, a stupid boy. It is too pathetic to think about; his life is ruined now,' said Allison.

'Well, yes, it is, but he still has a life. He is not lying in a hospital bed fighting for it,' said Amber.

'True, but...' said Allison.

'But nothing, that little shit-faced, self-inflated dirt bag put Robert in here. Don't forget that Allison. Don't go soft on him. We still don't know what the repercussions of his actions are on your and Robert's life. You said yourself that we won't know anything until he wakes up,' said Amber.

'I'm sorry, Amber, how are you doing? Did you manage to find everything that you need? Did you sleep well? Have you eaten?' asked Allison.

'I did sleep very well, thank you, your apartment is lovely. Baby is well and woke me up kicking, then I ran to the toilet to throw up, then I called Woods, he was hungover but still says hello... let's go for coffee, and by coffee, I mean hot chocolate,' said Amber.

FIFTEEN

Waking the next morning, Meg was aware of Ralph's breath warming her. She could see his expectant face in her mind's eye before she opened her eyes, his tail thudded on the bed. He knew she was stirring, her head hurt, and her mouth was dry, yet she smiled at the thought and feel of him staring at her.

She opened one eye; he made contact, and the thuds got louder. Awake, she scruffed the back of his ears, followed him to the kitchen, and opened the back door for him. The morning sun attacked her goodwill, and she retreated back into the kitchen in search of paracetamol and coffee. Meg saw that there were three empty wine bottles on the kitchen counter. She didn't remember opening the third.

She sat at the kitchen table and drank her coffee while she waited for the Panadol to kick in enough to help her to get moving. Ralph was back and hoping for a walk, but he knew her routine and that he would have to wait until she showered before they went. He was patient with her even when some mornings, like today, she took a little longer to get herself organised.

After a walk Meg walked the fifteen minutes to the nursing home alone while Ralph snoozed contently on the couch.

'Morning, Mum,' she said as she entered her mother's room. She hoped that today would be a good visit.

'Morning, dear, how are you? It is so lovely to see you, it has been such a long time.'

It had only been twenty-four hours since her last visit. 'Yes, Mum, sorry, I have been working.'

'Oh, that's nice. Where have you been doing the yoga? The women here are terrible. I keep telling them to get you in here, I say my Megan is a wonderful teacher.'

'Thanks, Mum. I have been working at the men's prison on a yoga rehabilitation program; it is going really well.'

'Well, that is lovely, dear. You might meet someone you can reform.' She giggled.

'Fancy a walk around the gardens today? It is a beautiful day outside,' said Meg.

'Oh, no thank you, dear, my daughter will be here to see me soon.'

And there she went again. 'How about we go into the garden and wait for her? I think they want to clean you room and make it nice for your visit,' said Meg.

'Okay, dear, if you have nothing better to do, let's go to the garden.'

Back home Meg caught Ralph napping on the couch. He knew he was not in trouble and thudded his tail against the cushions as she rubbed his black head. She made a cup of tea and headed to her study. Last night she had been very productive apparently, though the third bottle had dulled her memory somewhat. On her pin board reserved for yoga poses and meditations she had created a complex, visual representation of Scott Clarke's life, from what he had told her about his childhood, the information she gathered from social media, to the crimes chronicled in the media. She had somehow in her stupor managed to order transcripts of Scott Clarke's court case, making a considerable dent in her already suffering credit card.

Meg decided that she should write to Scott. He was her inspiration and could be the start of a new direction in her career. She owed him that much, and besides he had nothing else to look forward to. It was the least that she could do.

Dear Scott,

I am sorry that I didn't write to you last week, something happened that kept me distracted all week. It seems like a lame excuse now, but well...why don't I explain myself. I went out with my friend Charlie; we haven't caught up in years and we have been friends since school. Anyway, we didn't even make it into the club when I ran into my ex. Andrew left me a couple of years ago, a few bad things happened for us close together. My mum moved into a nursing home—she has MS and now early stage dementia, we fell pregnant, we lost the baby, stillbirth. He got offered his dream job researching something in the artic, said we were too much to bear, and left. I bought myself a Rottweiler from the dog rescue, Ralph, and have lived day to day in my mother's house since. In the back of my mind, I always thought that we would end up together. This was just a hiccup. Then he tells me he is on his stag do, he is getting married to some girl that he met at work, so at the Artic. Anyway, I know it was useless, but nothing worked last week. I mean, I didn't function too well. I cried the last of my tears and walked away from the hope; that is what I mourned, when it really comes down to it, I mourned the loss of the hope that I carried. Sounds so stupid when I say it out loud.

Now to your question, no, I don't agree that Bikram Yoga is ideal for anyone, that is my personal opinion. Hot yoga will just dehydrate you, and that is not good in the long term. I do Hatha or Ha-tha. A good book to read is Patanjali's Yoga Sutras. I will bring you a copy to class, do you think that anyone else may be interested? I could bring a few different books each week to swap around. I will check it out with the guards when I next visit. If they give the okay, I will bring a box load every week. I cannot see the harm in sharing yoga. That aside, I will bring your book with me this Friday. I also have a yoga mat for you. I will bring both this week.

Once again, I am sorry for letting you down last week, please know that it wasn't you it was my life temporarily falling apart over a stupid dream.

I am looking forward to receiving you next letter.

Namaste, Your Friend, Meg.

Done, Meg folded the letter three times, slipped it into an envelope and addressed it to Scott, then both she and Ralph walked down to the post office, stopping on the way back at the bottle shop drive thru for two bottles of tonight's solace.

Meg was awakened in the middle of the night by sounds of Ralph whimpering. Her head was foggy from the wine. She called his name; his tail thudded limply at the sound of her voice, but he didn't move. He only lifted his head and whimpered.

'Oh my god, Ralph, what is it? You will be okay, boy, I promise you.'

Meg threw a jacket over her pyjamas and ran out barefoot to open her car's rear door and started the engine. Back inside she gathered up the bedspread beneath Ralph, and in one lift she has him up and across her shoulders. He whimpered again but didn't fight her. She lowered him onto the tailgate of her hatchback and turned to work him into the car using the blanket as a pulley, dragging it through to the front of the car to pull him all the way inside.

She drove to the local vet, but it was closed. She called the emergency number and was sent thirty kilometres away to the all-night emergency vet. They must have called ahead for her, because when she pulled into the driveway of the carpark two men were waiting to carry the sixty-five-kilo rottweiler inside.

On the way one introduced himself as Dr Evans, the other as Michael, a vet nurse. They didn't mess around. Ralph was taken directly to surgery. Once his vitals were taken, he was intubated and given anaesthesia.

Meg held his head, talking to him and reassuring him that was the best boy and that everything would be okay. She felt him give her the weight of his head to hold and rested him gently on the operating table before bursting into tears. The vet nurse was at her side, a comforting arm around her shoulders.

'Please, I am okay, please concentrate on Ralph. I don't know what I would do without him. Please fix him, please find out what is wrong with him.' She stroked Ralph along the forehead and muzzle, tracing his markings with her finger.

'You may prefer to wait outside. Come with me, I will get you a cup of coffee,' said the nurse, placing two firm hands on Meg's shoulders and gently turning her away from Ralph.

Meg did as she was instructed and followed the nurse to the waiting room.

'He will be all right, won't he?' she asked.

'Yes, he has a very good chance. He is young, you brought him in quickly, and Dr Evans is an excellent surgeon. How about I get you that coffee?'

Meg sat for four long hours, thumbing through her contacts looking for someone to call. The sun was going up outside; the roads were slowly getting busy as commuters made their way to the city for work. She could hear mumbled voices behind the surgery door. It was good, she thought; *They haven't given up on him.* Another hour she sat, watching the world wake up outside through the glass shop doors of the vet's waiting room. The day staff began to arrive. One is quick to fetch her another coffee, then finally the surgeon came out.

'How is he?' she asked without waiting.

He took a seat next to her and explained. 'He had, as we suspected, a twisted bowel. We were able to remove a section of bowel and it looks good. He will need to stay in for a week, but I am sure that he will make a full recovery. You will be able to see him now. He is sleeping and will be kept sedated for a couple of days. It is important that he doesn't move around, but you will be able to visit him, pat him, talk to him. I believe that they hear us, know that they are loved and wanted, and it results in a better outcome.'

Meg followed the vet into the recovery room. It took her breath away to see him lying there on the table, tubes in his mouth, and a drain coming out of his stomach. The doctor explained about the tubes, but she didn't hear, she just listened to the sound of the machine breathing into his black, velvet muzzle. She stroked the outline of the markings around his head and kissed his soft nose.

'He will be okay, won't he, doctor, I mean after he has rested and healed? I will take him home?'

'Yes, of course you will. Now I am going home after I explain his care to the day duty staff, and I suggest you do the same.'

'Yes, thank you,' said Meg.

On her way out the receptionist stopped her. 'Meg, we just need to discuss the bill with you. Unfortunately, it is my job to break this down for you.'

'Okay, no worries, of course. Sorry, I wasn't thinking,' said Meg.

'No worries, you have had some night. Anyway, the total bill comes to four thousand, eight hundred and seventy-five dollars; that includes the seven days we require him to stay in hospital because of the abdominal drains and so on.' The girl placed the bill on the counter in front of Meg so that she could read it through for herself.

'Okay. Can I sort it out this afternoon, please, I need to go to the bank. He has pet insurance too,' she said.

'Yes, that is good, but we do need payment in full, then you can claim it from your insurance company. Again, we won't be able to release him until the bill is paid in full. I am sorry, I know it is a lot of money.'

'Yes, thank you. Like I said, I will be back later today,' said Meg.

Meg got into her car, relieved Ralph was fine, but *fuck!* *Where am I going to find the money?* She checked her online banking: seven dollars and eighty-three cents overdrawn, and her credit card balance was over-limit. She called her credit provider to ask for an increase and was declined within three minutes. Having no other option, she drove her car into the first car yard that promised her cash for cars. They would give her six thousand right there for her car. She took it and ordered an Uber to take her to the bank, deposited the bank cheque, and was told she has to wait five working days for the cheque to clear. She was running out of cash, but she got paid in the morning for her prison class. Meg walked the three kilometres back to her house, lugging the contents of her car with her.

At home she showered, dressed, made herself a coffee, and walked to the nursing home to see her mother.

'Good morning, dear! How are you, Meg? I have not seen you for ages,' she said.

'Mum, it is so good to see you.' Meg hugged her mum, grateful that today she knew her.

'Tell me, what is happening with you?' her mother asked.

'I had to take Ralph to the vets last night, he needed surgery. I just sold my car to pay the bill. I don't know what I am going to do. Mum, I need to find more work. But I have an idea to get more work at the prison.'

'Oh, I don't think there will be any need to go to prison, it was your car, you can sell it if you want to and don't let anyone tell you anything different. Poor Ralph, he is such a sweet little pup.'

'Yes, he is bigger now than when you last saw him. I wish you could see him. Here.' Meg brought up a picture of Ralph next to her on her phone and showed her mum.

'Yes, I remember him, and you, and all the times we had. Are you looking after my tomatoes?'

'Yes, mum, I am. I will bring you some tomorrow, and the strawberries are fruiting too now,' said Meg.

'Good, yes, that will be lovely. Perhaps we could make some jam and have afternoon tea in the garden. I would like that. What do you think?'

'Yes, Mum, I would love it. Let me see if I can organise it with the nurses to take you home for tea.'

'No, dear, they won't let me go. Do you know they lock me in at night? They won't let me go. I like strawberry jam, and they won't let me have any.'

'Mum?'

'No, dear, I think that you have me mixed up with someone else. Perhaps you have me confused with Elsie, some people say we look sisters.'

Just like that her mum had gone again. On her way out Meg stopped and talked to a nurse, who agreed that the moments where her mother was lucid and aware of herself were fewer and fewer. She reminded Meg not to argue with her mum, just to play along. It was the same conversation she had with many adult children, just play along, they trained her to say; it doesn't do any harm. And it didn't do any harm to the elderly residents of Sunshine Village. They didn't know, but the hurt you could see in the eyes of their children, it returned some to rejected primary school-aged children, to be denied recognition from their parents. It didn't matter that it was unintended, it still hurt.

Meg walked home, unsure where to turn. She rang Charlie and left an upbeat message on her message bank, not wanting to sound pathetic but feeling it all the same. She stopped into the bottle shop and used the last of her cash she could buy a couple of bottles of cheap wine, one for now and another for tonight. Tomorrow she would have her wages, tomorrow she would be okay. And next week Ralph would be home, and she would be okay.

She sat at her computer with a glass and wine bottle.

Allison Songbird was on the news again, smiling, surrounded by friends, supporters, everything she needed. Her beautiful man was in hospital, so all bless Allison, pray for Allison, bedside vigil, blah blah. Meg printed off the latest pictures of Allison and added it to the board next to a picture of Robert on an ambulance gurney next to her. Meg linked the image to the people that Allison knew that had died. *Really looks like you are a jinx, Allison Songbird.* Meg poured herself another glass.

SIXTEEN

Allison met with Robert's medical team. At their invitation, she sat in a chair across a broad, polished table. They exchanged niceties. She accepted the glass of water offered and took notice of the tissues nearby.

'We want to talk to you about the direction of Robert's treatment,' said the man seated across from her, she didn't recognise him from the ward. He went on and explained to her that Robert needed to be taken off life support again. They needed to know that he was a viable survivor.

'What the fuck does that mean?' she asked.

'If he can breathe and function on his own. There is a significant chance that he has sustained irreparable brain damage, that he will never wake up,' added the grey-haired doctor seated at the end of the table.

'Then we keep the machine on until he wakes up,' said Allison.

A woman in a pantsuit spoke up. 'I am sorry, but we need to consider the alternatives. What are his wishes, what were his limitations as to how and in what condition did, he want to be kept alive? Does Robert have a will? Have you both discussed this?'

'No, we never thought that we would have to, who does?' said Allison.

'I know, I understand,' said the doctor that had treated him, speaking for the first time. 'What has happened here is a tragedy, and we really don't have a definitive path to take. What we know is that if there is to be any hope for Robert to survive this in any capacity, he must be capable of breathing on his own.'

'What do you mean, any capacity?' Ally asked.

'We do not know how his brain has been affected or what the repercussions of his attack are. He could wake up and with a bit of rehabilitation overcome the last month in bed and he will be fine. He could wake up and have no memory of past events, or no short-term memory; his motor skills could be affected; he may never wake up. Today, in this meeting, we need to know what plans you and Robert have for such a situation.'

'We have no plans for this. We were about to start a family.' She rubbed her hands across her forehead and down her face. 'I am sorry, I do not understand what it is that you want from me. I know that all I want from you is that you keep him alive.'

Allison got up and left the room and made her way back to the seventh floor and Robert's room, sat at his bedside, rested her head on his chest, and cried. 'Robert, you must wake up, I can't do this on my own. Please show us a sign that you are there, that you can hear me, Robert....' She sobbed into his chest that rose and fell under the pressure of the machine.

'What is happening,' said Amber, walking into the room.

'They want me to decide on an end-of-life plan for Robert. They say they need to take the tube out, that he has to breathe on his own to be a viable survivor.'

'What the fuck, that is bullshit. I will go to court, get an order, and make them keep the machine going,' said Amber.

'No, I don't think they intend to do anything without my approval. They wanted to know if he had an end-of-life plan. I said no, of course not, we were planning a family, not this.'

'Okay, do they want to take away the breathing tubes like they did last week and see if he is okay to breathe on his own again?' asked Amber.

'Yes, that was it, just to see if he is okay, otherwise what is he? What kind of life would he have?'

'Not the life he wanted, I am sure of that. But how do they know, he could wake up tomorrow? He could be lucid, and breathing, and happy to be alive,' said Amber.

'Yes, but what they are saying is they don't know how or when he will wake up, how damaged he will be, his memory, his motor skills, his everything. It all begins with a breath, with him taking his own breath. I don't know what to do.'

'Ally, have you checked that Robert doesn't have an end-of-life plan? He is in the forces and, well, both Woods and I have one. They advised us to draw one up when we signed up. Maybe Robert has one, but like you say it just hasn't come up before.'

The morning began as any other day. Scott woke in his cell at five in the morning, rolled out the yoga mat that Meg had brought for him, and went through his practise, hearing her voice as he inhaled and exhaled. He was feeling stronger. The poses were becoming easier for him to get into, and he could hold them for more breaths each time.

When his practise was done, he sat down to write some more to Meg. He was trying to give her a blow-by-blow account of his day, live, not recounted like usual. He remembered to tell her it was her voice that guided him through his practise, that he was feeling stronger and better daily. He was walking more upright, more proudly, and he held her personally responsible. Scott wanted Meg to know that she meant something, that she was useful, that she was important. After what that Andrew did to her, she needed to hear it from someone.

At seven the cell doors opened, he left his cell and went to the communal bathrooms. They were usually quiet around then, and he preferred it. He was the first there and took the stall farthest away from the door, turned on the water and lathered himself. He felt good today. There was less pain in his body, he was healing.

Then it came. A thud across the back of his head. Another to the back of knees. Followed by a flurry of blows. Scott couldn't hold up his slippery, sudsy body and lost his footing. He was on the ground curled in the foetal position in an effort to protect himself. The water splashed in his face. Bars of soap held in prison socks pelted into his skin. Scott didn't make a sound. He knew they wanted to hear him whimper, so that they could tease him about the noises he made later, the begging and crying he heard from other prisoners returned tenfold to the victims in the canteen and out in the exercise yard. After the beating, they wanted to humiliate you.

They finished when their arms tire. He was unconscious. He was no fun now, there was nothing more to gain from the beating. 'No fun here, boys,' said the ringleader, and they left Scott Clarke, curled under the water, bloodied suds gathered around his body.

Late that afternoon, Scott awoke in the infirmary. There were stitches above his eye where a fresh bar split his skin on impact. His broken nose back was taped back into place. The skin along the side of his exposed body glowed with purple, tight skin engorged with blood.

'Well, hello again, Mr Clarke,' said the prison doctor. 'Didn't you take half a good battering. Soap in a sock, I see. Could have been worse, son, they could have taken a fancy to your arse too. I would thank my lucky stars if I were you.'

'Yes, thank you for fixing me up again, Doc, it has been a while. How is the family?'

'Well, you know, life with teenagers and a menopausal wife could never be easy.' He laughed. 'How is your pain? I gave you a needle when you came in, but that could wear off anytime now. I should give you something to help you make it through the night. Nothing to it but rest, I'm afraid, but I can keep you here for a few days. Make sure you are comfortable. I will bring the chess game tomorrow, how does that sound?'

'Great, doc, I miss our little games.'

'Me too, no one else has ever stayed in here as much as you. Here, drink this water, you will need it. The pethidine will dehydrate you, and the last thing you need is another episode of kidney trouble.'

Scott did as the doctor ordered. 'You are all right, Doc, a decent human being. I know it was you that got me on that yoga program. It is the best thing that I have ever done. Meg, the instructor, is helping me with a daily practise too, to help loosen my back. It is really helping, and I have to say I was feeling on top of the world when I woke up today and did my practise. Then I had to take a damn shower and those kiwi boys got me,' said Scott.

'You would think that this prison would have enough of beating up on you,' said Doc.

'No, I deserve it, I know I do. What I did was terrible. I cannot pretend otherwise, but I couldn't help it. You see, I would just meet people sometimes, and I know that they have to die. I guess that is the same for them when they meet me, and they just know that I deserve to be punished. Then there are other people in the world like you and Meg, that extend a kind hand to me, and I know that I have to honour it, and be decent. I don't know why. Can I tell you something? I have been trying to work out what the difference is between Allison, who I would still kill given the opportunity, and Meg, whom I adore and would happily die to protect. Two women, both talented, sure, both kind and both good people, except I despise one and treasure the other.'

'Well, it is true that different people affect us in different ways. It can be anything that gets us going, the sound of a voice, the shape of their face, the turn of a phrase. Hell, not that long ago and in some places still the colour of another person's skin, or the god they believed in, was enough to incite hatred, bloodcurdling hatred. I don't know that you are a bad person, Scott, I only know you as I have found you, and that is to be courteous, good-humoured, intelligent, and wise for your age. I do not condone or understand the things that you have done that brought you here and I won't pretend to. The Scott Clarke that I read about in the papers was and is a monster. The Scott that I know is someone that, had we met in other circumstances, I would have a game of golf with, followed with a few drinks in the clubhouse. I would invite you to our Christmas party. Most people keep their evil locked up inside, like Jekyll. You didn't. Which is why you are in here.'

'That is the truth,' said Scott.

'Here, you need to get some rest, and I have to go home. We are having Martha's roast for tea tonight. Why don't I bring you a plate in for your lunch tomorrow? I will ask her to make me two lunches.' He winked and pushed the drug into Scott's IV tube.

'Thank you, Doc,' said Scott.

In the early hours of the morning Scott awoke alone, stiff and sore. He struggled to get himself upright, but when he did, he adopted tadasana, mountain pose. He breathed in and heard Meg's voice soothing him through each breath, each inhalation and each exhalation. He attempted a forward bend but returned himself to standing when the room spun. Today it satisfied him to be a mountain, breathing in and out. Strong and proud despite his malady, he thought to himself that he must remember to tell Meg how she helped him in even the darkest of situations. He knew it was important, somehow, that she must know what a difference she was making in his life.

His right side was weakening, and he could feel himself fading. He repositioned himself on the bed, fixed his blanket, and realigned his drips. With his head supported on the pillow he let the sound of her voice take him through the neck rotations, then followed his body down to his feet practising Yoga Nidra. When his hands came to rest on his belly, he was tired and reverted to watching his breath and let the feeling carry him back to sleep.

He was woken later that morning by a guard. 'Clarke, wake up, you have a visitor.'

'A visitor.' He rubbed his eyes. 'Who? I don't get visitors,' said Scott.

'Today you do, make it quick; she has to be in class at ten,' said the guard, motioning for Meg to enter the ward while he cuffed one of Scott's hands to the bed.

'Meg, wow, this is a surprise,' said Scott.

'How are you doing? The guard told me you wouldn't be in class, and when I asked them why they told me what happened,' said Meg, pulling the visitor's chair closer to his bed.

'How is Ralph?' he asked.

'How are you? Look at you! What happened?'

'Just a routine pelting in the shower; it looks worse than it is. Once the swelling settles down I will be back to my cell and work as usual. Tell me, how is Ralph?'

'He is fine, resting at home. I have to sedate him when I come out, but he is doing great. Thank you for asking.'

'I felt so sorry for you both when you told me. He is

lucky to have you. Few people would sell their car to pay for surgery. You truly are special, and I bet he knows it too.'

'He is a wonderful dog. I would be lost without him.'

'Then I am glad you have him, you deserve him. Listen, I want you to know that your yoga is with me all the time. I wake and practise, I breathe at your command. You truly are a gifted teacher. Thank you for coming here. You have changed my life.'

'Thank you, that is nice of you to say so, but here, I have brought you some books, you can read them while you are convalescing. These are my favourite all-time yoga books. I think that these will help you understand where I am coming from.'

'Thank you so much, Meg, I will enjoy reading these since the prison library system is a little scarce on yoga books.'

'Sorry, Meg, it is time to go, the class is lining up,' said the guard from the door.

'Thank you, I am coming. Take care of yourself, write soon, and I will hopefully see you next week. If you're up and mobile, still come along even if you have trouble moving around, and I can take you through some breathing exercises. Your colour is frightening,' said Meg.

'I will be okay. Doc is taking good care of me here. Namaste, Meg.'

EIGHTEEN

Walking through their apartment for the first time in weeks, Allison entered their bedroom. The sheets were rumpled from their last time here, together. She held his pillow to her face and remembered that day, how he surprised her by coming home early, how she had the joy of waking up with his arms around her. She missed him. Tears flowed and dampened his pillow. Spent, she laid it down and made the bed.

In the closet Allison found the box of paperwork they kept for 'just in case'. The box contained an assortment of insurance papers, warranties, receipts, certificates and their wills. She hadn't looked at his, and truth be told she never asked about it. They never discussed end of life matters beyond the fact that they were both organ donors. She wondered now if that had been the right thing to do. Did other couples discuss this? She only knew Amber and Woods, and they did. Were they just being foolish in ignoring the possibility?

She held his last will and testament in her hand. It was

sealed. Allison wanted to open it, but she suddenly felt paralysed. Opening this could put an end to all her hope, destroy their future, and kill the man that she loved.

'Is that the letter?' asked Amber.

'Yes, it is his will. I can't open it,' said Allison.

'Would you like me to open it? Ally, it needs to be done. I wish there were another way,' said Amber.

'I know, me too. But it is the what ifs. How can I be sure that the doctors are right?' said Allison.

'All we need to do now is open and read this document. It may not even contain any end of life instructions, it may just be his will. That will make you his legal guardian, and then it is up to you whether the hospital continues to intubate him. I do understand how hard this is,' said Amber.

'Okay, please open it,' said Allison, closing her eyes and hanging on to the image of Robert on the morning of the day he returned home.

'Okay, well, I am surprised there is no end of life statement, just a will, and all it reads is, 'I leave everything I have to my dear wife, Allison, except for the trust I have established for my son, Joshua.'

'What? His son? I didn't know that he had a son. What the fuck? When do you suppose he was going to tell me? Joshua? Amber?'

'No, I didn't know either. He didn't even come up when we did a background check on him years ago,' said Amber.

'Do you mean he had an affair? Is this son the result of an affair? Is that why he couldn't tell me? When, where. Who?' asked Allison. 'I can't believe this, I thought I knew him. I thought I knew everything about him. I trusted him, and now he is as good as dead lying in that hospital bed and I find out this,' Allison cried.

Amber took her in her arms and led her friend to the bed.

'Here, lie down, rest, and I will give Woods a call. He can do a rush search on births in Western Australia over the last two decades, then at least we can establish a time frame and you will know. I don't believe he cheated on you; he is so in love with you. He rotated his entire life around you and the service. Robert is a good man, this didn't happen while you two were together.'

'But, Amber, what if you are wrong, what if he did? What if he met someone, they at least had sex once if not more, a relationship, whatever, that happened behind my back, while I was busy having a career. He may have done this. He could have cheated on me. Men cheat all the time.'

'Allison, steer yourself away from that road. We don't know, and there is no point thinking bad of the man yet. Believe me, I would help you kill him if this happened while you two were together,' said Amber, leaving the room to call Woods.

When Amber returned, she found Allison in the walk-in closet, boxes of shoes and papers at her feet. 'What are you doing?' Amber asked.

'There must be something here, some clue, something about this kid. You do not set up a trust for just anyone; this is his son, it has to be. My husband has a son, and I fuckin' well want to know where, and when he appeared, then why, *why* didn't he tell me.'

'We will know when soon. Woods is on it, and he agrees with me, Robert is not the type of man to have an affair, he loves you way too much,' said Amber.

'Did he? How do I know, Amber, really, how well do we know anyone? We give our hearts and bodies to our partners, our husbands, and do we really ever know what goes on in a man's heart or mind? How do we ever know that we ourselves are enough? How do you know that they never desire another woman, longer legs, bigger breasts, blonde hair, brunette hair, no makeup, more makeup, slut, saint, housekeeper, party girl, how the hell do we ever know that we are the one, the one woman, that will satisfy their everything? The woman that they won't stray from—and it doesn't have to be an affair, it could be a desire, an online fling, watching other woman they find more interesting than you online, it could be anything. We are never safe, and after Gavin, another nice guy that would never cheat on me but fell fast into an office affair within a heartbeat of me leaving, my point is you never know. Do you really know that Woods is faithful, one hundred percent to you?' asked Allison.

'No, I don't, and yes, sometimes he has questionable internet history, but I love him. Maybe I am not every woman he has ever desired or will desire, I am tall and boyish, I have to work to be womanly and feminine and yes, I get sick of it. I love it when he is away on assignment and I can slop around in trackies and baggy t-shirts, no makeup, no effort. But I know he loves me. I know he is more hands on when I make an effort to dress nice. No, I don't like that he looks at porn sometimes, I don't really understand it, and I know all men believe all men do it, but they don't. Some men think about their partners first, think about how they would feel if the situation were reversed, those men would rather commit murder than hurt a woman they loved. We all want that man.'

'Yes, and I thought I had that man,' said Allison.

'We all do, and you still might. Don't judge him too harshly yet. It may not have been an affair. Just be pissed off for now that he did not tell you before. We will know soon,

Woods has dropped everything to sort this for us,' said Amber.

'Tell him I said thank you. I do appreciate you two in life. I miss us living so close. If this isn't the end when Robert wakes up I think we should talk about moving back to Perth, sharing a simpler life and having play dates with you and Woods and the babies to be,' said Allison.

'That's the spirit, forward planning. That's Woods.' Amber answered her phone, walked towards to the window that overlooked the city, mumbled *thank you*, and hung up.

'Well, what did he say? When was this Joshua born?' asked Allison.

'Good news is that Robert never cheated on you. Bad news is that the mother of the baby is Robert's sister-in-law, and Joshua is nineteen, which means Robert was only sixteen when he was born.'

'Oh, well, that explains why I have never met his older brother. He said they had a falling out years ago, and I am guessing this was it,' said Allison.

'It may explain too why he never told you. Chances are that he wanted to, but he couldn't risk you being disappointed in him. He obviously did the wrong thing sleeping with his brother's wife,' said Amber.

'Wow, were they married at the time?'

'It appears so. The mother's name is Jacinta Williams. What do you want to do now?' asked Amber.

'Honestly, I want to go through his old photos, his computer and phone looking for links to Joshua and to look for photos. There must be something, a photo that he kept, something somewhere. Do you think that Joshua ever knew that his uncle was his father? I wonder where he lives.'

'You can't see him, Allison. Wait until Robert is on his

feet again, then you two can discuss how best to handle this news,' said Amber.

'You are right, now that I know he is just a secret keeper and not a cheating, lying bastard, I should get back to the hospital. I will talk to the doctors again and ask for a second opinion. Why don't you get some rest? You look tired, Amber. Thank you for your help, for being here.'

'I am glad I can be here for you, and yes, if you will be okay. I wouldn't mind a nap. I will come tonight and have dinner at the hospital with you,' said Amber.

On the ride back to the hospital, Allison searched through photos on Robert's phone. She hadn't done it before and was surprised to find the number of pictures of herself sleeping, saved from the internet, and of her on stage. She followed the photos back years through his history. There were no old girlfriends, nothing. Even his internet browsing history gave her nothing to think that he was not the man she loved and trusted. He really adored her. His calendar showed how he counted the days until he would be home with her. He loved her, she was sure of it. If Amber were right, Allison could see how shame would stop him from telling her about Joshua. He broke his brother's trust, and he wouldn't forgive himself easily for doing so.

Sitting next to his bed, she held his hand as she waited for the doctors to arrive on their afternoon rounds. When they did, she informed them that there was no end of life document, and that she wanted a second, independent opinion. They agreed it was the correct course of action to take and promised to send Robert's medical history and their findings to any doctor of her choice so that when he or she came to examine Robert, they would have all the information at hand.

Not knowing who to call or where to find a doctor for

Robert's unique condition, she took out Robert's phone and called his commanding officer. His commander had promised that they would have a team of medical experts look over his file and send the people to examine him by the end of the week. It was only Tuesday, so she had bought Robert a few more days on life support. She could only hope that he would wake up in that time.

NINETEEN

Meg woke in the early hours to Ralph licking her face while his tail thudded on the bed.

'Hey, boy, you seem happy, are you okay? Do you feel better?' Meg asked.

He nuzzled into her, wanting his broad, black, velvet head stroked.

She hugged him. 'I am so glad that you are okay, boy. I would be lost without you.'

She got up, put on the kettle, and he followed her to the back door. She lets him out into the cool morning chill, sat on the step, and watched him sniff and assess the garden, trotting around with his new lease on life. He came back to her, sat at her side, and together they watched the sunrise.

Meg was determined to put Ralph's convalescing time to good use. In her study she had established two boards: on one side there was the story of Scott Clarke, as much as she could put together from social media, mainstream media, and things that he had told her. On the other side she had been working on a program to take to prisons across the state for yoga for rehabilitation. She was nearly set to compile a prospectus, but first she would have to run an official, documented trial at Casuarina.

Ralph was whining, looking out of the window, and giving her all the signs that he wanted to take a walk. 'Okay, boy, it doesn't do you any good to be cooped up in here, but just a slow walk, okay?'

His tail thudded the wall as he waited for his leash. She walked him down to the nursing home. Her mum was in the yard, sitting next to an elderly gentleman she hadn't seen before. Meg waved to her, and her mum waved back, perhaps more out of politeness than recognition. Meg felt positive today. It was going to be a good day. Ralph was healing, her mum looked happy, and her work was on track. No more crying over Andrew.

Ralph slowed his pace on their walk home. He had his breakfast and some medication for the pain, since his tummy was still tender after the operation. He laid on her study floor at her feet, wagging his tail with contentment, and soon fell asleep. Meg kissed his nose, and he roused enough to wag a bit more as she left to visit her mum.

She found her mother sitting alone in the garden. 'Morning, mum.' She bent forward and kissed her cheek. 'Morning, dear.'

Meg could already sense that it was going to be a good visit. 'Would you like to take a walk around the garden or are you happy to sit here?' asked Meg.

'Oh, Meg, I think a walk would be lovely. Do you mind pushing, or should I call a nurse?'

'Of course, I don't mind. I am happy to, it will be my pleasure. You seem in good health today.' Meg took the brake off the wheelchair and manoeuvred her mother onto the walking path.

'I am. I have a delightful new friend, Harrison, he just

arrived the day before yesterday. He is in a room near mine. I will miss him when I go home. Perhaps he could come and visit. I have told him all about your dog, Ralph, and he is very fond of dogs. In fact, he used to have a German shepherd before he came here, the dog is with his son now. Maybe we could arrange a play date?'

'Between the dogs, or you and Harrison, Mum?' said Meg. Knowing that it would never happen she played along, grateful to see her mum happy and acting like herself.

'Well, that will depend on whether we can get you out of the house, won't it, Meg.' Her mother laughed.

'I am sure I can find an excuse to clear out and leave you two alone, if that is what you want, Mum. I would love to do that for you,' said Meg, holding back a tear, remembering how vital her mum used to be and all the things that they used to do together.

'Tell me, Meg, when are you and Andrew going to finally get married? It would be a fun occasion, and I could bring Harrison as my date. And besides, isn't about time you two got on with it? I am not getting any younger, and I would like to see some grandkids before too long, and you deserve to be happy, dear.'

'Thanks, Mum, but Andrew is away in the Artic working. Maybe when he gets back, we will set a date. We have just been too busy up until now.'

'Stop that, Meg, stop saying that you are too busy for life, for love, for children. Live your life today! It goes so fast —one day you are running, the next you need help to get out of bed. Run, Meg, enjoy your life while you still can. Take it from me, it is no fun sitting in this contraption and meeting a man you could romp with and knowing you can't, that you missed your chance because your body has aged and betrayed you.'

'Okay, Mum, I will. But tell me, how is physio going? Perhaps they can help you with mobility. It may not be the same as when you were younger, but Harrison looked like he can move around well. Perhaps there is a way you two could get it on,' said Meg, smiling and hoping sincerely that it was true.

Back at home, Ralph greeted her at the door, then her phone buzzed a message from her bank that she had received the eighty percent insurance money back from her pet insurance.

'Woo hoo, boy, I can buy another car.' Meg buzzed herself an Uber, and in no time, she was on her way back to the car yard where she had sold her precious Suzuki and hunted out the salesperson. Meg asked him for the best deal he could give her on a similar car. Two hours later she pulled back into her driveway in a wagon, picked up Ralph, and took him back to the vet to have his stitches removed.

That night it felt that all was right in her world. She poured herself another glass of wine and cut an article out of *The Australian* featuring Allison Songbird and the ongoing saga of her knocked-out husband.

TWENTY

Sitting next to Robert in the hospital and holding his hand, Allison thinks, *why didn't you tell me. Were you ashamed? I hope not. After all the things that we have been through together, I would hope that you could tell me anything. Please wake up, Robert, I need you; I need your voice, your ears, your guidance. Your touch. I do not know how I could negotiate this world without you.* His hand rested limply in hers. The machines were doing the work of his lungs while a monitor beeped in rhythm with his heart rate.

'Hey, Allison,' said Amber, entering the room with a shopping bag and two cafeteria coffees.

'What have you got there, something for the baby?' asked Allison.

'Yes, look, I bought it from the gift shop, couldn't resist,' said Amber. 'Look, it is a little superhero romper, and look, a rescue pet teddy and look, a bag of violet crumbles he will have to eat through me.'

'Violet crumbles. I like the way *he* rolls...do we know the sex? I never asked, sorry.'

'No, we didn't want to know. I am just assuming that the amount of kicking I endure and my recently enormous appetite for just food that it is a boy. How else can you explain it?' 'Do you have any names picked out?' asked Allison.

'No, we haven't gotten that far yet,' said Amber, passing Allison a fresh cappuccino. 'Here, have a crumble.'

'Thanks. I don't know what I am supposed to do, Amber, I want him to live and wake up, be here. Why did that boy do this?'

'Honestly, all we know is that he was just big noting himself in front of his friends, showing off on the tail end of a drug-induced night out. Chances are that he was still on a high, that he thought he was being funny and tough. We know he was weak; it was a shit thing to do. I went to his pre-trial hearing this morning. He was there in a suit, private school blazer and all. The parents have him lawyered up and banging on about what a good boy he is with a bright future, *blah blah*, heard it all before from parents that believe their kids are better than anyone else. They think that they just got in with a bad crowd, that this wasn't like them. "No," they say, "my little angel couldn't do anything so monstrous." But they can, and at some point, they have to accept it, that their little darlings are arseholes. I saw that moment in court today, after their lawyer did his, "Oh, but your honour, jail time would ruin a promising future" speech.

'The prosecution stood up. "Your honour," he said, "I am here to speak for the victim, an officer in the Australian Air Force, just returned from serving his country on an overseas mission, to see his wife for the first time in a very long time. They were out celebrating being together, enjoying a dinner out, a dance, like any young couple would hap to do. They were walking home along the bridge path, to their new home, having recently moved from Western Australia to have a better life together, and the accused saw fit to cut their night short. The victim now lays in a hospital bed, on a respirator, with no signs of recuperating, a promising life cut short, a dream of two people ended; two responsible, hard-working, valuable people just starting their lives together hangs in jeopardy." So, that said, the judge remanded him into custody with a court date being set when Robert has recovered.'

'And if he doesn't recover?' asked Allison.

'Then he will be charged with murder,' said Amber.

'None of that helps Robert, but I am glad that he is not getting away with it. He doesn't deserve to. He should suffer too.'

TWENTY-ONE

It was yoga day, the doctor had given Scott permission to attend after sending Meg an email with some information about his condition. Half his body was bruised and battered. It was going to be hard but beneficial for him to move around, but it was important to aid his recovery. The doctor mentioned he knew Meg would understand and be thoughtful of his condition throughout class. He knew because of the things that Scott had told him.

Scott had spent his mornings that week working on a modified sun salutation, moving slowly he worked with both sides of his body, using his bed for support. It impressed the doctor that Clarke cared so much about his rehabilitation. Meg had been a beneficial influence, and that was what these men needed. Why else would they want to rehabilitate?

Scott waited at the locked door to the newly named yoga room. He had come straight from the infirmary on the doc's permission without a guard. He heard the sounds of Meg being escorted through the locked gates towards him. He did his best to straighten up and fix his hair.

'Scott, how are you doing?' She smiled when she saw him.

'Better, thank you. The doctor said I should be okay if I take it relatively easy during class today. I have been practising, and it helps,' said Scott.

'I know, the doctor emailed me this morning, said that you would be in class, that he thought yoga would be good for you. I am glad you are here. I have brought you a bolster. It is being looked over by the inspection guards now. They said they will deliver it to you later today. It will help you manage the poses.'

'Thank you, that is really kind of you,' Scott said.

They both turned to the sounds of the other men coming down the corridor.

'Let's get this show on the road, folks,' said the guard, speaking for the first time and unlocking the room.

Meg entered first, Scott followed and unrolled his mat. He inched his way down to the floor using his good arm for support. Meg noticed the pain across his face and glimpsed the purple bruised flesh just under his shirt. The other men nodded an acknowledgement to him as they took their places.

He placed his hands lightly on his broken torso, inhaled and exhaled lightly. Scott knew he had to expand his ribs, keep his lungs and muscles moving to keep himself going. It hurt, but he tried not to wince. He could sense that she was watching him, assessing his movements, his abilities, seeing what he was capable of.

He followed her voice. Eyes closed, he pretended they were alone in the room, and no one else existed not the walls, the locked doors, the guards, the barred windows. No one else, just him and Meg, that voice reminding him to breathe, to stay alive.

His mind drifted to his most recent beating, his breath shortened. In the distance he heard her voice, and she brought him back to the room, back to his breath. He was grateful for her.

When class was over, he thanked her, and she handed him a piece of paper with some diagrams of simple yoga poses he could practise with the bolster the guards would leave in his cell. He thanked her and left with the other men. He asked the guard if he could return to his cell. He didn't feel he needed to take up any more of the doctor's time. He explained, 'I just want to get back to my routine, my work, my yoga.'

'Sure,' said the guard. 'I will let the doc know. Watch your back, Clarke; it may not be over, and we can only do so much.'

'Thanks, I know.'

Back in his cell he dusted off the surfaces of his desk and drawers, checked his bed for surprises glass, bugs and the like and lay down on his bunk. He wouldn't be on library duty for another week, and that was fine. He had a lot to think through.

'Here, this is from Meg. She said it will help you recover. Not sure how, but she knows?' The guard stood at the door to his cell, holding the teal bolster.

Scott stood slowly and took the bolster from the officer. 'Thank you.'

'Christ, they really did a number on you this time,' said the guard, shaking his head and walking away down the corridor.

Scott lay back on his bunk, holding the bolster at his side. Took the piece of paper from his pocket that Meg had given him. Smelled the paper and heard her voice in his ear.

She looked good. He must write to her; he would close his eyes for a minute, rest, then he would write.

It was dark when he woke and the door to his cell was locked. The prison had already shut down for the night. He had slept right through lunch and dinner. The bolster was still in the crook of his arm. He rose and listened to the sounds of night in the prison: the breathing, snoring, and nightmares of the other prisoners. Rising from his bunk he went to the toilet, washed his hands in the basin, washed his face, and took a drink of water from the tap. In the darkness he rolled out his mat, took hold of his bolster, and inched his way through the exercises that Meg had given him. He let the sound of her voice guide him. Across their divide, she taught and encouraged him.

When he finished, he could feel the loosening in his joints, the calm in his mind. He pulled out his notepad, and in the dim light that came through his window from the yard lights, he wrote Meg a letter.

Dear Guru,

Thank you for your class today. I came back to my cell and fell asleep. Here I am now in the middle of night. I have just gone through the exercises you left me with the bolster, and I feel amazing. Thank you. You really know what you are doing. I am so grateful for what you have done.

Tell me about Ralph, how is he, is he better? He is so lucky to have you take care of him. Can you send me a photo of him? Growing up, I had a dog, a bitsa, a large bitsa. We called him Boof. He was pretty cool. We would play fetch and the sight of him would scare the shit out of some people. His bark was deep and powerful, but I guess with Ralph the Rotti you would know all about that. I remember the huge dinner Boof would eat; it was incredible to watch, and yet he was so gentle with babies and little animals, you know, kittens and chickens. He followed my sister around everywhere from the moment she was born. He would defend her against everyone, even Mum and Dad if they tried to tell her off for something. He would stand between her and them and growl. Then one day, he was just gone. I am not really sure what happened. No one ever really told us. Parents are odd, the way they try to hide things from you. All they are really doing is teaching you how to accept being lied to.

I haven't been able to read the book you sent me yet, I have been sleeping all day. I wonder what you are doing now...sleeping, I guess?

Will you keep coming to teach us yoga? It really is helping me and the other guys, I am sure. No one complains about coming like they used to at the first class. You shut everyone up.

I want to ask you something else, and it is okay if you say no or if it is not appropriate., I would like to talk to you. I would like to sit face to face with you and have a proper conversation; about yoga, you, Ralph, your mother, anything really. I feel drawn to you, connected in some weird way. If this it too much tell me, I will not mention it again, but I think you need to know. When someone matters to you, you should tell them. Don't let it disturb you, I am still a man, I am bound to be attracted to you and I am, but it is more than that. It is more than the fact that no one else on the outside knows me, bothers about me, or even remembers my name, never mind takes the time to think about my wellbeing, to write to me to encourage me to feel better. Thank you, I really appreciate all that you have already done for me, and if you don't want to visit me that would be okay or if you can't because you simply do not have time to visit me, then I will understand. I do not want you to feel obliged to me. I am and always will be very grateful for anything that you do for me. I don't deserve a person like you in my life in any capacity.

I am warbling; the hour I guess, but I think I should be clear up front and maybe you would like to be invited? Again, you can always decline, you can always say, No, Scott pen pals and yoga classes are enough. That would be okay, I promise. What you have already given me is more than I deserve, and I thank you, and will be eternally grateful.

With the greatest appreciation and respect,
Your friend and loyal student,
Scott Clarke

Scott folded the letter into three, slid it into an envelope, and addressed it to Meg.

TWENTY-TWO

'Well?' said Amber, entering Robert's hospital room for the the first time that day. 'What did they say? What was second opinion? Robert is going to be okay, isn't he, Ally?' Amber sat down in the chair across from Robert's bed, feeling the bile rise in her throat.

'No, they say that we should take out the breathing apparatus and then re-examine him then. Until he is breathing on his own, they can't or won't say. There is some brain activity, but not as much as they would like to see. They don't know, Amber, no one knows,' said Allison.

'What is this?' asked Amber, gesturing to the papers on Robert's tray.

'The forms to sign him away to the unknown. If I sign this, Amber, he could die,' said Allison.

'Or he could live. I have read that there is a school of thought that says coma patients under stress are more likely to build resilience, improve brain activity, and recover sooner. It is possible that when having to do the work for itself, the body switches into survival mode more readily. But it is just one school of thought. We know

Robert would not like to live like this. This is not a life,' said Amber.

'I know, but what if it is not enough time, what if his brain and body need more time to heal and to recover to wake up on his own? Are there any studies that say the mechanical breathing apparatus was switched off too soon, the patient could have lived if only he had a few more days, a week, a month a year? Amber, I know that this is no life, but where there is life, any glimpse of life, surely there is hope. If I let them turn machine off too soon, before he is ready, I could lose him forever.'

'God, Allison, I don't know what to tell you, I know that if it were me and that was James, I would do anything to keep him plugged into whatever machine he needed, for all time. He isn't in any pain? And of course, you are right. Where there is life, there is hope. I worry they will try to put pressure on you here. Don't do anything that doesn't feel right; it has only been five weeks,' said Amber.

'Five weeks? It doesn't seem like it has been that long, and you, poor Amber, you have been away from Woods...and the baby, oh wow, that belly of yours keeps growing. You need to be home, before it is too late for you to travel,' said Allison.

'I can't leave you like this. We need to get Robert sorted.'

'Well, it doesn't matter what they say here, and I don't know why I am even contemplating their advice, thankfully there is an alternative. The Australian Air Force has a veteran's hospital just outside of Sydney. I can have him moved there. They will not stop the intubation while they can still track signs of life,' said Allison.

'Brilliant, maybe next time lead with that. What can I do to help you?' asked Amber.

'Go home, nest, do what pregnant women do. You can't have the baby here away from Woods. You two need to be together, and I will be okay. I know it is just time that Robert needs, time to heal, and he will get it in a hospital away from the city and the attention of the media, away from the pressure that is put on him here to heal.'

'I don't feel right in leaving you,' said Amber.

'If I need you for anything, and I call you, will you come?' asked Allison.

'Yes, you know I will, I can be here in a day,' said Amber.

'That is enough, that is all that I need to know, that I can call on you. You have already done so much. I can take it from here; you need to get ready for that baby.' Allison hugged her friend around the shoulders. 'I called my agent. She has booked you a ticket for the flight back to Perth tonight.'

TWENTY-THREE

Meg arrived early Thursday morning. Sitting in her car outside of Casuarina Prison, she breathed deeply. The sun was already high in the sky, and the heat of the day was setting in. Meg scooped up the stack of yoga books she had brought, reminded herself that this was a good idea, and climbed out of her car.

At the gate she told the guard she was visiting Scott Clarke.

He raised an eyebrow. 'He will be surprised,' he said, buzzing her through and directing her through security.

The visitor's room was cold, the air conditioner was set to a temperature more suited to later in the day. Her skin was goose bumped as she took a seat at the cement table bolted to the grey, cement floor. There was a window on the south side with two guards watching her. She wondered what they must think. Did they think her a manipulated fool? Was she? Or was she just a nice person trying to help a person in need? She slid the books along the table closer to her.

A guard walked Scott into the visitor's room. He smiled

when he saw her, despite his bruises, awkwardness in movement, and the cuffs between his hands and ankles.

Meg smiled in return. 'Hello, Scott, how are you feeling today?'

'Meg.' He took a seat across the table, and the guard secured him to it via a hook.

'Is that really necessary?' Meg asked.

'If I do this, I can depend on the men in the watch room to keep you safe; otherwise I will have to sit here between the pair of you and interrupt your privacy,' the guard explained.

'Meg, it is okay, you are safe, and we will be able to talk. I don't mind, they could wheel me in here on a fridge trolley Hannibal Lector style, I am just so happy that you are here. Don't worry about the chains. These are mine, not yours,' said Scott.

'Okay, as long as you are okay, I can live with it too,' said Meg.

'Well, hallelujah,' said the guard, closing the door behind him.

'I can't believe that after all this time you are actually here. Talk about what you have been doing since the last time you wrote. How are Ralph and your mother?'

'Well, mum has a boyfriend. His name is Harrison. He used to be a sea captain, and now he is spending his day wooing my geriatric, partially demented mother. It is sweet really. Even though there are days when she doesn't remember him, he keeps trying, he will just pretend that it is the first time that they have met. He is very patient. I even suggested that he keep a diary for her, like on *The Notebook*. Have you seen it?'

'No, I don't think so. He sounds nice. It must be an enjoyable time in life, you know, when all the hard work is done, when you have finished with trying to be somebody and build a life, a career, a family. All you have to do in old age is to endure, and live to endure another day, and hope that you have a bit of joy along the way. I think it would be a delightful time of life,' said Scott.

'Yes, I can see when you put it like that that it would be a good time of life. When you put it that way, it is nice. I feel better when I leave her, knowing that someone is looking out for her. You know, other than the staff, he is more invested in her wellbeing.'

'I can see how you would feel that way. It must have been difficult for someone like you to have put your mother in a home,' said Scott.

'What do you mean, someone like me?' asked Meg.

'You are so caring and worried about other people's wellbeing. Look at you here, helping me, a monster trialled by media, a heartless criminal if you are to believe the press. Yet here you are trying to help me,' said Scott.

'I know what you did. I have been looking you up, and, well, that is what you did. That is not who you are, and to that end I only know who you are to me, that is all I can judge you on. My mother always taught me to take people as you find them. That is how I will see you. I worried because of what is happening in my personal life that I was using you as a distraction, I would end up one of those women I read about once in a doctor's surgery magazine, that marry their pen-pal prisoner boyfriend, love behind bars and all that. I am not planning on that. I can give you friendship, and I am more than happy to help you with your yoga, but that is all. I need to know that you understand that.'

'I do, and I wouldn't ask anything of else of you. I am very grateful that you take time out of your life to think about me. Thank you. It makes my life easier to endure,' said Scott.

'Phew, I am glad we got that out of the way and we understand each other. Tell me, how are you feeling?' asked Meg. 'Better. It's just bruising and broken ribs, and I am healing. Faster, I think, with the exercises you gave me, and that bolster. It is amazing,' said Scott.

'How do you recover from that, mentally?' asked Meg.

'I deserve it, Meg. It is my penance, it is how I earn my place back into the world. The people that did it feel like they have exacted some punishment on someone that deserves it, like they have brought some justice into the world. So it is win-win,' said Scott.

TWENTY-FOUR

Allison woke up to a gurgling sound he was making.

'Robert?' She pressed the buzzer for the nurse. 'Robert, I am here, it is okay, they have you intubated, don't panic. They told me to tell you not to panic.'

The nurse came through and checked his vitals. 'Welcome back.' She double buzzed on the call button, a sign for the doctor to be called.

Robert's eyes opened. He couldn't quite focus, and his throat hurt. He had a feeling of choking. He could hear Allison and knew that there was a nurse in the room, but he couldn't see anyone clearly. He couldn't speak; his words come out in grunts. He wanted to tell Allison he was okay, he could hear her, but he couldn't say a word, he could only grunt.

'Hello,' said the doctor, leaning over his face. He shined a light in Robert's eyes.

Robert winced, the brightness hurting his head.

'It is okay, we will get you up and about soon. You have been sleeping a long time. I need you to take a deep breath.' The doctor put his hands on Robert's stomach. 'Now breathe out; I am going to pull on this tube. It will feel as if you are about to throw up, but it will be okay. The more you relax, the easier this will feel.'

Robert nodded in understanding. He did as the doctor instructed and coughed up the tube being pulled through his oesophagus.

A few more checks and Robert was encouraged to drink on his own. He cautiously took little sips of water.

As suddenly as he woke up and his room filled with activity, he and Allison were alone.

'Oh my god.' She wrapped her arms around him.

He lifted his own arms to hold her, they felt were heavy and weak. He kissed her as she smothered his face with her kisses, wet from her tears.

'Hey, don't cry, I would never leave you. What happened? Where am I?'

'You are in the military hospital. I had the air force's medical team move you here after the Sydney General Hospital was going to remove your breathing and feeding tube. They promised you could take all the time you needed here. I love you.'

'How long have I been here?' asked Robert, taking in the room, the cot, the pile of folded clothes and the vanity next to Allison's cot, the cards, the books.

'Eight months,' said Allison.

'What? Eight months! Have you been here all that time? Sleeping there?'

'Yes, where else would I be?'

'What about your album, the concerts, the tour?'

'What about them? Robert, you are all that matters. I couldn't take the chance of you waking up alone, needing help and not being able to call for the nurse or doctors, or worse still stopping someone turning off your machine and

leaving it to chance that you could function without them.'
Tears were flowing down her cheeks.

'Oh, Allison, I am so sorry I put you through all this, but
I am here now. We can get back on with our lives. Tell me,
what has been happening?'

'Well, Amber was here, she stayed for eight weeks, but
she had to go home because her and Woods were having a
baby! She is pregnant, well, was pregnant. They now have a
beautiful little girl. She is a few months old now, here.' She
showed him a picture of the baby on her phone.

'She is beautiful. They are very lucky. It is nice that she
came over to be with you. It must have been awful,' said
Robert.

'It wasn't great, I won't lie, a lot of things have
happened, but the most important is that you are awake and
coming home soon.'

'Soon? Can't I come home today?' Robert asked.

'I don't think so. The doctors said that when you woke
you would have a lot of muscle atrophy and would need
physio and occupational therapy. It could take a month or
more.'

'Aren't you sick of being here?' asked Robert.

'Yes, of course I am, but there is no rush. I have put all
my work off for a year, and I would have done so for longer
if you still needed me here. I couldn't leave you, and now
you are awake and have a voice, you can look after your own
needs a little. Soon I may go back into the studio and work
on the album, but I plan to be here a lot until we can go
home together,' said Allison.

'It sounds like you have it all planned out,' said Robert.

'Yes, I do. I have done a lot of writing and thinking
about us and what was going to happen when we were back
together. We need to get you healthy, and, yes, you are right,

I need to work for myself too, and while I planned on a year, singing keeps me sane. You understand, don't you, Robert?' Allison asked.

'Yes, I am sorry if I sounded difficult, I didn't mean to. I am tired and a little confused about how and why I am here. I feel weak.' He looked down to his legs and squeezed his thighs. 'What are these? It's just flabby skin, where is my *oomph?*'

'I know, that is what the rehab is for. You need to build your strength up,' said Allison.

'I think that is where I come in.' A man in a polo shirt and track pants entered the room. 'How are you doing? I have been looking forward to meeting you. Your file has been on my desk for months. Nice to see you awake. Welcome back. My name is Gary, I am here to help you work on getting your strength back and moving around on your own. I will get the nurse to come and remove your catheter, and then I will be back in an hour for your first walk to the bathroom. It will give us an idea of where we are, and then we can talk about where you want to go.' 'I want to go home,' said Robert.

'Yes, of course you do, and it is my job to get you home and back to feeling like your old self again.'

Gary left them alone, carrying Robert's file and talking into his mobile phone.

'He seems nice,' said Allison.

'Ally, how long have I been here?' Robert asked.

'The attack was eight months ago. Originally you were in Sydney General, then I had you transferred here, Robert, I told you this, remember?'

'No, I don't. Why can't I go to the toilet on my own?' asked Robert.

'Robert, Gary just told us it is because of muscle

atrophy that your body needs to build back up from scratch. It won't happen overnight, but you can get there. Would you like me to get the doctor back in?'

'I haven't seen the doctor, have I?' asked Robert.

'I will call him now, Robert.'

'Allison, I am scared.'

'You will be okay, Robert, it is probably just a normal response, you have been asleep for a very long time. I will speak to the nurse and ask for the doctor. Close your eyes and rest. You have already done so much today, and you will start your physio soon.'

Allison kissed his forehead.

Robert closed his eyes and took a deep breath. Outside in the nurse's room, she met the doctor and explained that Robert seemed to lose his short-term memory and told him how he had forgotten things she had already just told him.

'I am sorry, Allison, this can happen sometimes, and you would not like to hear this any more than I am telling it, but it could go away today, next month, in a year, or never. There is no way of knowing until he is out of it. We don't know.'

'I know, I know, I just want to make sure that there is nothing we can do?' Allison asked.

'I have scheduled Robert for an active brain MRI to confirm that there no residual brain injury. In the meantime, keep talking to him, not about anything too important, and try to be patient, he has a long way to go. Don't you let him lose hope. It's important, even if you feel like a broken record. One more thing, I see you have been staying with him every night. I know you have a life outside of these walls, a career and commitments that you have put on hold, my wife is a big fan. Now is the time for you to step back into life a little. Take time out for yourself. We will take good care of him.'

'Thank you, doctor. I have spoken to him about doing so. I would like to return to the studio and hash out a bit of work, now that I know he will be okay.'

'Good, and I will speak to the occupational therapist about his memory. They always have some new tricks up their sleeve to whip out for a patient in need. Go sing and try not to worry.'

She smiled, thanked the doctor, and took herself for a walk to the cafeteria. Without his memory, there was no point asking him about his son. He would go around in circles, and it could upset him. *On the other hand*, she thought, *what if he forgets I brought it up and we could bury it between us and move on with our life?* It didn't sit right. She couldn't decide what to do.

She ordered herself a coffee and took the carrot cake from the shelf, paid the cashier, and took a seat by the window. Outside it was raining. A man with a young boy was running in from the carpark carrying a bunch of flowers and an enormous bouquet of balloons. A father and son. Robert could have been the father and that his son. He deserved to know his son. They couldn't sweep him under the carpet. But she would have to wait.

She took a forkful of her cake, rolled it around in her mouth, and washed it down with a sip of coffee. This was her daily lunch. Today was the first time she had sat outside of the hospital room, watched the sky and listened to the sounds of human interactions; not the hissing, beeping of machines and the drone of daytime television. *Yes*, she thought to herself, taking another scoop of cake, *I have to sing, make music and be part of the world.* Allison would stay with Robert while he was doing his rehab. She could get her career back off the ground. She called her agent to get the ball rolling; she was excited to hear from Allison and promised to text her all the details of upcoming events, studio times, musicians, and interviews that were backing up. She rattled off a load of names Allison didn't recognise and promised to send her a schedule soon.

Next, Allison called Amber to tell her the great news and coo over the baby on face-time.

Back in his room, Gary gently woke up Robert.

'Hey there, sleepy head, I am here to take you for an all important walk to the bathroom. The nurses have given me this for you to fill. They need to measure your output, make sure they keep you hydrated. Take your time, and when you are ready swing both of your legs over here to the side of the bed.'

Robert shuffled his bum up to sitting and moved his legs to the side of the bed where they just hung, limp and exhausted. 'That was ridiculously hard. I feel so weak and look so pathetic. This is not the body I came in with,' said Robert.

'No, it is not the body that you came in with, but this is the body that we have to work with. This is our starting point. We will have you jumping and running out of this place! Now, put your hands on my shoulders and use me as a walking frame. This will not be easy, but we are going to go to the bathroom.'

'Okay. Where is the bathroom?' asked Robert.

'There.' Gary gestured. 'It is just three metres away from your bed. I don't want you to attempt it on your own for the next couple of days.'

'Are you shitting me? This can't be who I am.'

'It isn't. You are a man, well-loved and important to this world, that suffered a pointless attack, that fell into a coma, and now is being given time and opportunity to rebuild himself. You can make yourself strong again. That is why I am here, to help you now, and I will be here until we are done. Okay?'

'Okay, sorry. I must sound like a pathetic whiny brat. I don't mean to, it is just...I woke up to find my life has been on hold, the woman I love has put her own life on hold just when her career she fought so hard for was taking off, and we have lost eight months together, all for what? I have spent so many years fighting in the service of my country and nothing ever happened to me, then *bang*! Some idiot king-hits me and takes a period of my life away, and I am left with this weak, pale body. I used to be strong.'

'Then be strong, in your mind first, your body will follow. Trust me, we are all here to help. Don't be afraid, but you will be discouraged, you will wake up tired. Your limbs will ache and be sore from training. You will feel like you can never make it back to being your old self. You will cry because it will be hard, you will cry because you are afraid of never fully returning to being the husband you once were before all this happened to you. But I need you to remember to hang in there. I will be here for you every step of the way, and that beautiful wife of yours will be there for you too.'

'How can you be so sure?' Robert asked.

Gary lifted his pants legs to reveal two prosthetic limbs. 'Afghanistan. I came home half a man. I didn't think my wife would want me, didn't know what job I could do, what use I could be, what was the point of having kids, how could I be a father, how could I even make love to my wife. But I did my physio and cried myself to sleep. I did my therapy, I studied to be here, I loved my wife, she was patient and showed me what our new marriage looks like. Now we have four kids, I work here, and I train my boys' soccer club. My life is worthwhile, but I had to walk through fire to make it so, and so will you. You love your wife, she loves you, your lives will go on together. This, my friend, is just a hiccup, a small blip on the road map of your life. Now hold my shoulders and stand up. These legs of mine can take anything; they are one hundred percent titanium.' He smiled and nodded at Robert to do as he was told.

With a hand on each of Gary's shoulders, Robert lowered his feet all the way to the floor. His feet felt like bags of flour as he placed them on floor and tried to lift himself up.

He failed, voicing his frustration. 'I can't do it.'

'Really, I think you can, and you should. I expect better from you, captain,' said Gary.

Robert looked him in the eye.

Gary knelt lower and lifted Robert as he tried to stand, stayed with him, and when he was steady, took two tiny steps backwards, enough to extend Robert's arms. 'Now, follow me,' said Gary.

Inch by inch the two shuffled to the bathroom. A sweat broke on Robert's forehead.

Words of encouragement came from Gary. 'Well done,' he said as he helped the panting Robert position himself on the toilet. 'Place a hand on the rail. I will give you some privacy now. It may feel strange; this is your first time going to the toilet in over eight months. I will just be outside. Call me when you are done. I am here to help you, mate.' Gary left Robert alone with the door opened just a crack so he could hear if he were needed. He jotted down some notes on the progress made so far and waited for Robert to call him.

TWENTY-FIVE

Meg took Ralph along to visit her mum and Harrison. It was a fresh, spring day, and she was keen to get on with it. Ralph strutted at her side, his tail wagging faster as they approached the gates of the nursing home. Her mum and Harrison met them in the garden with tea and cakes prepared.

'Well, this is all so lovely,' said Meg, taking a seat at the table.

'Today is a special occasion. Your mum has agreed to be my wife, with your permission of course,' said Harrison.

'Of course! Why on earth would you need my permission? That is wonderful.' She stood up and kissed them both congratulations.

'It means we can have married quarters,' said her mum. 'Here, Ralph, this is for you.' She handed Ralph a piece of beef jerky she had kept especially. He gently took it from her and laid at her feet to eat it.

'Okay, when and where will we be having this wedding?' Meg asked.

'Here, in the garden, we thought. All our friends are

here, and the staff can help us arrange things. What do you think?'

'I think it is wonderful. I can take photos, I know a cake maker and a dress maker. Mum, Isobel can make you a beautiful wedding dress, and flowers; let me sort those out, Mum loves gardenias,' said Meg.

'I do, thank you, dear, it is all very exciting, isn't it? And you will bring Ralph, and of course that nice young man you are seeing, Scott? It will be lovely to meet him.'

'Yes, I know he will love to come if he is not working on assignment. He can come and celebrate with us another time. I know he would love to,' said Meg. 'What about catering, should we get something brought in?'

'What do you have in mind?' asked her mum.

'Well, how about first we sort out a guest list, then we can fish around to find out what our options are?'

'I think we will have to invite all the residents, even the ones we don't like. There is so little celebration here, so little goes on, it would be nice to involve everyone. Perhaps we could surprise them, you know like a surprise party, so we don't have too many busy bodies interfering in our planning,' said Mum, tapping the side of her nose.

'I understand, we will just have to clear it with the staff. They can help us set up the area and get people to the ceremony,' said Meg.

'Let's do it three weeks from now, I don't want to waste another second,' said Mum.

'Okay. It is so very exciting,' said Harrison.

On her way out of the nursing home, Meg stopped in the nurse's office to discuss the planned nuptials. They were delighted and supportive of the union and agreed to help them on the big day.

'I am worried,' said Meg, 'about Mum's memory fades. What if she forgets on the day?'

'I have noticed that your mother's short-term memory has been improving, Harrison helps her and seems to be able to talk her back. She is less afraid with him at her side. It is lovely to see. She will be fine, and better off too for having someone at her side, and we can all see that he adores her,' said the head nurse.

Meg walked Ralph home a little lighter in her step at the thought of her mother finding love at seventy-eight, in a nursing home. It was wonderful, a fling was alright but why shouldn't they spend the rest of their lives together?

At home she re-filled Ralph's water bowl and fed him his breakfast of chicken mince, rice, and veg, that he devoured in less time than it took her to walk to the bathroom. She showered and dressed while Ralph snoozed on her bed, rubbed his head, and kissed his muzzle goodbye before heading off to the prison to see Scott.

At the prison she went through the routine of emptying her bag, going through the metal detector, body scan, and answering the same series of tedious questions. With the addition on one more, the guard added on for his own interest, 'What is a girl like you doing, mixing with a man like Scott Clarke?'

'I do not know the Scott Clarke that committed those crimes. I know of them, I know to some extent what drove him to those things, but I don't know that man. The man I know is kind, intelligent, spiritual, and fun. He also needs a friend, and that is why I am here,' said Meg, loading her things back in her bag, ready to take the next step through the gates and into the visiting room.

She sat down at their usual table and pondered the

morning so far. When Scott shuffled in, attached to his shackles in his prison jumpsuit. She was bursting with news and hugged him quickly as the guard left the room.

'Well, my lovely, you look happy,' said Scott.

'I am, today is visiting day, and you will never guess what my mum is up to,' said Meg.

'Let me guess, she is running away to join the circus?'

'Ha-ha, no, better, she is getting married to Harrison. Can you believe it?'

'Oh well, that is wonderful. Not only will she have someone to keep her company in her aging years, but Megsy will have a new daddy,' he laughed.

'Hilarious, but you are right, he takes wonderful care of her. I feel better knowing that she has someone else looking out for her.'

'It makes a big difference to your quality of life to have someone that cares about you. I know what a difference you have made in mine. I smile every time I think of you. You mean the world to me, Meg, I mean it when I say I love you.'

'I do too, Scott. Any word about your re-trial?' asked Meg.

'No, and I don't think the lawyer they sent me is taking it too seriously. So many preconceived ideas get in the way of people wanting to learn the truth. I wish I had met you sooner. I wish I could live my life with you. While I am so grateful that you come to visit me, I wish we could have more. Be together, sleep with you in my arms and wake up to your smile. For real, not just in my mind,' said Scott.

'I would like that too. We have early parole to look forward to. I am not going anywhere, not now I have found you and I have a permanent contract here too, so it's a win for me.' Meg winked at him.

'Meg, marry me?'

'What?'

'You heard me, marry me, be my wife. Say you will, then we could spend more time together—they have a room set up for family visits, private, and we could be together. We don't have to do anything, just be together, without these chains and cameras and guards peering in the window. You could always divorce me if you meet someone on the outside. I would understand and agree willingly, I promise,' said Scott.

'Oh, shut up, yes, I will marry you, but how? Can we? Will they let us?'

'I don't know, but get yourself an engagement ring and start signing in as my fiancée. There must be a way we can be married. I will speak to the chaplain and the warden, maybe they can sort something out for us,' said Scott.

'I don't suppose they would allow us any guests if they let us marry here,' said Meg.

'No, I don't suppose they would. You don't have to. Am I asking too much? Just tell me if you are unsure, I know it is not the type of wedding a girl wants, and you really deserve so much better. I have no right to ask you. Please forget I said anything,' said Scott.

'No, I won't, and you were not wrong for asking me. I want to marry you, and I want to see you alone, in that room. You deserve a life too, and maybe having a wife will mean you get an early parole. I could fight for your re-trial. You will have someone, an advocate in me fighting for you on the outside and someone to come out for. You are allowed to be happy too, Scott.'

'There are plenty of people around that would disagree with you. I cannot believe my luck in finding you, in being with you, and now you are agreeing to marry me. It is romantic, isn't it?' asked Scott.

'Yes, it is. I will buy a ring, and next week you can propose to me properly, and then we can sort out how we are going to get married.'

They kissed quickly before the guards could warn them off.

On her drive home Meg stopped into the shopping centre's only jewellery shop and peered over the engagement rings. She chose a modest, zirconia diamond with a princess cut; it was only one hundred and eighty dollars on sale, so within her budget, and was ring enough to show that she was with somebody now.

Her phone buzzed. It was a text from Charlie saying they hadn't caught up in ages, let's have drinks this Friday. Meg put her phone back in her bag without replying. Weaving her way through the shopping centre, she thought of her impending marriage to Scott. How could she tell Charlie, or anyone for that matter? She wasn't ashamed of falling in love with him, but if she were standing on the outside, she understood how it could seem a little desperate, getting married to a man serving a life sentence. Where was the future in that? They could have conjugal visits sure, once a month if he behaved so they could also have children —that she would be left to raise alone, that would have to tell their friends Dad couldn't come to their school show because he was doing time. Was that a life? Did she even want children?

Stopping at the news agency she collected the latest tabloid magazines. Allison Songbird featured in everyone, "Wounded Husband Wakes from Coma", *hall-e-fucking-lujah*, Meg thought. Allison could have everything, and all

Meg and Scott wanted was a small taste, a small piece of what those two had. Meg's eyes narrowed on the smiling image of Allison Songbird staring back at her from the glossy pages of the magazine. The shine from her own ring caught her eye. *Yes, I am entitled to some happiness too.*

At home Ralph greeted her, and she told him the good news, then they headed to her office. Meg sat at her desk scouring the magazines. Meg tore out photos of Allison and Robert and pasted them into her growing volumes of scrapbooks. She used scissors to cut out the articles and pasted them next to each photo, then, taking her watercolour pencils, she drew patterns around the edges, nothing pretty, just squares or odd shapes repeating. She didn't want it to be pretty.

The last magazine she bought was a bridal magazine. Meg took it to her bedroom, and Ralph followed her there, jumping on the bed with her and nuzzling her hand for attention. She thought of her own wedding, the one she had in her mind as a girl: big, white dress; flowing, princess-style train, bloom upon bloom of white flowers in her bouquet, her hair, in the church and at the reception. She was to have someone sing her down the aisle and a ten-tier cake. Her wedding was not to be a paltry affair, it was to be an occasion that marked the beginning of her impending life with her beau.

None of that mattered anymore. She was in her thirties, she was in love, and really, she was old enough now to realise that love was all that mattered. Everything else was just fluff. She couldn't have fluff for her wedding if she could even have a wedding. She would take a marriage to Scott any way she could get it. Her mother, on the other hand, she could have all the bells and whistles that could be mustered.

Meg picked up her phone and dialled Charlie's number. It went to her message bank, so Meg simply said, 'It's me, would love to catch up, Mum is getting married, and I could use your help. Come over for drinks, pizza, and wedding planning on Friday if you're free.'

TWENTY-SIX

It felt good to be singing in the studio again. Allison felt herself coming back. She wished it was the same for Robert, it was hard seeing him struggling to find himself again. He had been so strong and sure of himself, and now he questioned everything, from what shirt he should wear to what he should eat for lunch. No one knew when he would be back to his old self, if ever. Allison just had to be patient and remember that he was her man, the one that she chose to be with in sickness and in health.

Pulling up to the hospital, she exhaled, paid the driver, and walked the familiar corridors towards Robert's room. She was tired. Work in the studio was going well, but it required all of her attention to keep going.

She changed direction slightly and headed to the cafeteria and ordered herself a salad roll and a green tea with honey. It would only take ten minutes, she told herself, and then she would see Robert. Perhaps he had a good day today.

As she sat there waiting alone, Gary walked through the

door to the cafeteria. 'Hello, Allison, mind if I join you?' he asked.

'No, it's fine, please do,' said Allison.

He ordered his food at the counter and took the seat across from Allison.

'How did he do today?' she asked.

'Better. We walked unassisted to the bathroom and used the frame to walk up and down the hallway. We practiced using a pen and played a few games on his iPad,' he said.

'Games, really?' asked Allison.

'Yes, they help with extending both his concentration, his memory, and dexterity,' Gary said.

'Oh, yes, I see how that could work,' said Allison. 'Sorry, I didn't mean to sound grumpy, I am just tired.' 'Tired of coming here?' he asked.

'Yes, and no, and yes, and from work and wondering when life will get back to normal, when I can speak to Robert properly, when I can ask him something, when he can come home, when we can be husband and wife again, living our life without all this,' she said.

'I know, and I understand. It must be very frightening for you, frustrating, and a few other "f " words you are free to throw around. I promise you that this will pass, and if you are still here, it will make for a stronger relationship,' said Gary.

'What do you mean if I am still here? Where else will I go?' asked Allison.

'Forgive me, but often partners of injured patients think that they have to stay.' He reached for her hand across the table and continued, 'that there is no alternative, when there is. You don't have to stay with someone if you are not getting what it is you need out of the relationship, no one would blame you for seeking comfort elsewhere,' said Gary.

Ally pulled her hand away. 'I hope you are not implying what I think you are but get this straight.' She stood, leaned her hands on the table, and levelled herself at his face. 'I love my husband. I would wait a thousand years for him to wake up, to heal, to be ready to come home to me. I will take him any way he comes, because he is my husband and I love him. You really need to tell me right now that this is just a misunderstanding, that I don't have to tell your supervisor and have my husband reassigned.'

'I am sorry, Allison, I meant no offense,' said Gary.

'Don't be a creep and hit on sick men's wives, it undermines your integrity.'

Allison left her salad roll and untouched tea on the table and made her way to Robert's room. She was a little flattered, but that jerk had jolted her out of her doldrums about having to spend so much time at the hospital. She opened the door to Robert's room to find him practising his squats at the end of the bed.

'Well, look at you, you have been working out really hard, well done.' She crossed the room and kissed him.

'Thank you. It is great to see you. I have done one hundred squats above my daily tally. I want to get out of here, Allison, I want us to go home,' said Robert.

'Me too. I am tired of coming here and sleeping over there on a cot, I am tired of all the damn interruptions and beeping and noise, but you need to get stronger, Robert.'

'Do I? I mean, can't I have this treatment at home? At least you wouldn't have to waste all your time coming here to see me, and I could be useful, I am sure, around the house,' said Robert.

'Yes, that sounds wonderful. I am really getting sick of hospital food,' said Allison.

'Here, come and lie down with me.' Robert lay on one half of the bed and patted the free side.

She took off her shoes, locked the door, and lay down beside him.

'You couldn't possibly know how much I have missed you.' She laid her head on his chest, it was softer than she knew it, but his arms around her were resembling the strength she had known. Allison lifted her head to kiss him. Soft butterfly kisses laid a trail on her forehead. Her lips found his. They explored each other's mouths. It was their first kiss in months, and each one inhaled the breath of the other.

Allison's hand ran the length of his body, worked her way toward the centre line. She skimmed past his hardness, the brief touch caused him to gasp, her hand found its way inside his track pants. The smooth silkiness of him excited her.

He kissed her deeply as she positioned herself over him. On top of him she shimmied out of her underwear, pulled up her skirt, and freed him from his pants. 'I've locked the door, but they will come and check on you soon. I can't wait for you any longer,' said Allison.

'I had no intention of stopping you,' said Robert.

Allison lowered herself onto the length of him and looked him in the eye, to see his face filled with ecstasy. 'I love you, Allison.'

'I love you too.' She lowered herself to kiss him on the lips. She could feel him move underneath her. His hands were on her hips, and as she lifted herself she rocked herself on him. She let his hands explore her body.

He was taking in every inch of her body, the fall, the rise, and curves of her, her hair bouncing as she rode him home. He could not hold on. She rode him in waves, and as he felt her orgasm, he exploded beneath her.

She leant forward and rested her head on his chest. 'I need you to come home, Robert.'

'Yes, please get me out of here, we have a lot of catching up to do.'

TWENTY-SEVEN

'Warden, you must understand, I am in love, she is in love, and we want to get married,' said Scott.

'Have you really thought through what you are asking of this young woman? Are you okay with the fact that she will give up her life for you?' asked the warden.

'Yes. I know I can give her nothing, but an idea of marriage with a conjugal visit occasionally, maybe children, that she would have to raise on her own, on the outside, that I could only see on family day. But again, warden, and I don't know how to stress this the most, we are in love. I haven't been in love before. I have used people, destroyed people, but with Meg, I want to protect her, love and cherish her, and most of all she makes me want to be a better man. That has to be enough for you to approve our marriage, she makes me a better man,' said Scott.

'Maybe, yes, but what will it do to her?' asked the warden.

'She will be loved, forever. And one day when I am out of here, she will be my resting place. I would not do anything wrong again because it would take me away from her and the love we have. I couldn't hurt her. I would kill myself rather than hurt her. Tell me what I have to do to get you to approve of our marriage,' said Scott.

The warden slid a paperweight around his desk mat. This was the first time he had ever been asked such a thing, and Scott was convincing. He had a solid argument. The warden knew prisoners needed something on the outside to rehabilitate for, and Scott Clarke was an important prisoner to rehabilitate. He would never be released the way he was, but maybe this way, maybe this Meg, had changed him. As much as he thought her to be the most foolish of girls, she had already taken the darkness out of Scott Clarke's eyes.

'Okay, this is what will happen. Your engagement will be officially recognised. You can have family visits with Meg providing you have earned the privilege through good behaviour. This will happen for a year. I want you both to see the chaplain in that time for his marriage assistance course so that you both understand and discuss the realities of a prison marriage and whether you should move to having children. After a year, if you are both still keen to marry, then I will sanction a small ceremony here in the prison followed by a brief, extended stay in the conjugal rooms. How does that sound, bearing in mind that it is the best I can come up with and you really have a lot of years left to spend here.'

'Thank you, that is wonderful. I will work hard. I will be the best prisoner you have had. I can't wait to tell Meg,' said Scott.

'Okay, it's all good, but please do me one favour and consider the girl. As much as she loves you, is it really fair of you to ask such a thing of her?' asked the warden.

Scott didn't reply.

The warden dismissed him. The guard's hand on his

shoulder indicated it was time to leave. Scott followed the guard through the corridors back to his cell. The words of the warden ran through his head. Was it fair to ask Meg to spend her life tied to him with little promise of a proper marriage until they were well into their sixties? To raise their children on her own, to sleep alone every night. Yes, he thought, he would love her, he could never bring himself to hurt her, he wouldn't leave her for someone else, he would adore her. Worship her. He could be the man that she deserved to have love her. He would be free one day, and, in the meantime, they could plan their future together. He would show the warden, he would show everyone. Scott Clarke was made anew by Meg. She would be his wife, they would live happily ever after, they would grow old together and take that trip around the world he always wanted to do and be free with her.

Lying on his bunk, the pictures of Allison Songbird stared down at him. Reminding him of the monster he once was. He took out his writing pad and a pen from his bedside table and penned a new letter.

Dear Allison,

How very brave of you to not screw up this letter and destroy it without ever considering its contents. I have been following you in the magazines these years past. I see that you have become the singer that you always wanted to be, married a man that deserved you, and faced yet another tragedy. I am not writing to gloat. My life is going surprisingly well here in Casuarina Prison. I have a view of the sky and have taken up yoga. Also, I want you to know that I forgive you. I hope you will return the favour.

No need to reply, I just want to get on with my
life without being haunted by your face.
All the best for the future.
Scott Clarke.

He folded the paper three times, placed it in an envelope, and addressed it care of Allison Songbird's agent. Then one by one he took down the pictures stuck to the underside of the top bunk, tore them into tiny pieces, and put them into the toilet.

When they were all processed in this fashion, he flushed her away.

TWENTY-EIGHT

It rained the morning of the wedding, so Meg drove her car loaded with Ralph, a wedding dress, flowers, and balloons the short distance to the nursing home. The activity room was a buzz of excitement with chairs being laid out, flowers from the grounds being arranged, and the general chaotic bustling that happens when too many people are trying to help. Meg smiled when she caught the eye of a nurse that quickly explained, 'The best-kept secret is out of the bag.'

Finding her mum in her room, Meg hugged her, and Ralph, allowed inside on this special occasion as he was to be ring bearer, licked her hand.

'Let's get you ready, Mum,' said Meg.

'Ready for what, dear?' her mum asked.

'You are getting married today, Mum, to Harrison.' Meg searched her mum's face for recognition.

'Am I? Has he even asked me?'

'Yes, and you said yes. You love him, and today you get to move into the married quarters together. Look, I brought you the dress you picked out, and a gardenia bouquet. Ralph is wearing his best bow tie,' said Meg.

'I can see, he looks very handsome. Yes, of course I remember now, the dress, it is lovely. Did you make it, dear?'

'Yes,' sighed Meg, 'I did. And it will look beautiful on you.'

Meg's mum walked down the aisle accompanied by her daughter and Ralph. They played 'Unchained Melody' as the bride grinned her way down the aisle towards Harrison. The two exchanged the traditional vows, kissed, and partied until two in the afternoon.

Following the cutting of the cake, the residents returned to their rooms for nap time. They moved the newlyweds into their own shared accommodation in the east wing to spend their first afternoon as Mr and Mrs napping together.

Meg and Ralph headed home together. She dropped off the car and took him for a walk in the park, then home for an afternoon of working on her scrapbooks of Allison Songbird. It stewed in her like a festering sore, that Allison had everything and because of her Scott was in jail. She loved Scott, and she had to jump through hoops to be with him, and there was Allison over there in Sydney without a care in the world, having it all. When she spoke to her counsellor earlier in the week, she asked if Meg was jealous of Allison. Meg had scoffed at the suggestion. She was not jealous, she didn't want what Allison had. It pissed her off. She couldn't have what she wanted because Allison was there first and took it away from her.

Staring now at Allison's photographs, the life journey Meg had drawn up of the highs and lows of Allison's life, it really did not seem justified to her. So, Meg's mind took her one more time around and around in circles, questioning the whys of Allison's life, comparing them with her own, and Scott's.

Meg got up and poured herself another glass of wine. She kissed the fuzzy head of Ralph sleeping on her bed and returned to the study. *What if,* she thinks, *in a parallel universe, Allison Songbird doesn't exist?* Meg pondered the picture it would create. Meg and Scott could have met on the outside. He would have been whole, not battered with a limp and sad. He would have still had the swagger she imagined he had, sure he was still handsome even with the broken nose. But he had lost so much of his life, their life, being on the inside. Now she would have to raise their children alone. Allison can be with her husband, all healthy and healed from the attack. 'Hero Attacked', the headlines read. Where was such sentiment for Scott and Meg?

Meg poured herself another glass of wine, walked back to her bedroom where Ralph is still sleeping, and looked at herself in the full-length mirror. 'Really, girl, you have let yourself go.' Meg poked at the skin on her face, pulled down the black, circled bags underneath her eyes, rolled her hair and held it back in a twist, raised her chin, posed duck face with a shoulder shrug. She lifted her dress above her head. Turned to the side, sucked in her tummy, and when that was not enough, she lifted it with both hands to make it flat. Her legs were dimpled, and when she took off her bra, her breasts hung like empty, pendulous socks on her chest. 'You really have let yourself go.' She takes another drink from her glass.

Meg thought of Allison. *She doesn't look a day older than the picture of her coming out of the courthouse after she testified and put Scott away in prison.* 'She must get help. I bet she spends all day at a beauty parlour, getting this sucked, tucked, vibrated, needled, waxed, and electrified.'

Meg didn't have the money for that. The best that she could manage was some homemade oatmeal scrub, a litre of Vaseline intensive care, a razor blade, and some tweezers.

On her way back to her study she stopped and got herself another bottle of wine from the fridge. 'We must be the same age, yet we look so different.' She took a black marker to the loose pictures of Allison she had scattered across her worktable, doubles she didn't want in her scrapbooks. She drew moustaches, spots, and glasses on the images.

When she couldn't take it anymore, she chugged the remaining wine from the bottle between sobs. When the wine was done Meg cleared the table with a swipe of her arm. 'I hate you, Allison Songbird,' Meg yelled. She staggered back to her bedroom and collapses face down next to Ralph. He moved his body next to hers and watched for her breathing.

It was dark when Meg woke to Ralph licking her face and whining. Then he lifted his head to bark. Between his yells she could make out the knocking on the front door, put on a robe and fumbled through the dark house. She lit the porch and saw that it was Charlie, here for pizza as arranged at the wedding.

'Oh, my god, you look positively radiant,' said Charlie.

'Ha-ha, any more sarcasm and I will shut this door in your face,' said Meg.

Charlie lunged through the door. 'Too late, I am here. Why don't you have a shower. I will make us a couple of gin and tonics, order a pizza, and get *Love, Actually* on Netflix.'

'Yeah, whatever, make yourself at home, I hope you brought gin for said tonics, I am all out,' said Meg.

'Yes, I can see why. Go shower,' said Charlie.

Meg saluted, turned, and headed down the hall to the

shower. She heard Charlie make a fuss of Ralph and then the sound of the back door opening. She smiled knowing that Charlie was taking care of them. She was a good friend.

Watching Ralph around the garden, Charlie ordered the girls pizza and a meat lover's crispy for Ralph, then she followed him back inside. Walking past the study, she could not help but see the mess Meg had created. She walked in to inspect and saw the notice boards, of her planned prison yoga gig, and the photos of Allison defaced strewn across the floor. She flicked through the scrapbooks that went from Scott Clarke's trial to the attack on Allison's husband and subsequent recovery.

'How are those drinks coming?' asked Meg at the door.

'Sorry, the door was opened, and I couldn't help...'

'*Snooping*, I believe, is the word that you are looking for,' said Meg.

'Sorry, Meg, I honestly didn't mean of intrude. I didn't know that you were such a fan girl of Allison Songbird.'

'I am not, and it is a long story. Let me get dressed, pour me that drink, and meet me in the lounge room, and I will fill you in.' Meg pushed past Charlie to get to her room and closed the door.

Charlie did as Meg asked and was waiting for her with Ralph on the floor next to her in the lounge room. 'Okay, I am ready. Here is your drink, now tell me what the fan girl art is all about,' said Charlie.

'I told you, Charlie, I am not a fan girl, it is the complete opposite. I know you will work for her soon, but I am still not a fan. Remember that I told you I was working the prison, running a yoga program for inmates that were targeted as those that would benefit the most from a mindful practise?' Meg asked.

'Yes, I do, but—' said Charlie.

'Well, one of my students if Scott Clarke.'

'I don't know who that is,' said Charlie.

'Yes, you do. He is the man that kidnapped and tried to murder Allison Songbird some years back. He is in my group. He wrote to me asking about yoga exercises specific for him, and, well, we became pen pals. Then I started visiting him, and, well, we are going to be married,' said Meg.

Charlie took a big gulp of her drink. 'Married? How? Is he getting out?' asked Charlie.

'No, I am going to marry him in prison. The warden has already approved it provided that we stay engaged for a year and take some dumb course the chaplain runs for couples like us, to ensure that we know what we are getting ourselves into,' said Meg.

'You mean so that you know what *you* are getting yourself into,' said Charlie.

'No, it is not all one-sided. Imagine marrying someone and raising a family with them and having to deal with all that you missed out because they locked you up inside and they were free to roam, travel, meet other people. That is a lot to deal with. Putting up with a marriage while you are on the inside,' said Meg.

'He is on the inside for a very good reason. Your own scrapbooks are evidence of that.'

'No, they are not. They are a snapshot in time. It was just a passing phase. He is not that man anymore, just like you are not that emo girl you were back in high school. Imagine if the black lipstick and nails were permanent and you were forced to rock that look now along with your linen and lace. People change,' said Meg.

'Murderers and psychopaths don't, Meg,' said Charlie.

'How can you say that? You don't know him, you

haven't met him, you do not know what he has been through,' said Meg.

'Black fingernails and lipstick are not the same as murdering another human, torturing an innocent girl, burning down Fremantle markets, and that is just off the top of my head.'

'He is not that man. I thought you would understand,' said Meg.

'I don't understand, how are you going to have a fulfilling relationship with a husband in jail?' Charlie asked.

'Well, I have yoga session once a week with him, and yes, nineteen other inmates. We are allowed to visit once a week and on family day, and once a month we can have a conjugal visit. I can keep working. I am working on expanding my program throughout all Western Australian prisons, so I can support myself, and if we decide to have children, I will be able to look after them too,' said Meg.

'You really have thought all of this through. Tell me why the pictures, the vandalised ones and the ones set out in your scrapbooks,' Charlie said.

'I have spent a lot of time coming to terms with the things that Scott has done. I wanted to know more about Allison. He had been so obsessed with her, even he can't say why,' said Meg.

'You are not trying to become like her, are you? He didn't ask you to be more like her and less like you, did he?' asked Charlie.

'Why are you trying to make this about something that it is not? Why can't you just accept that we are in love, that people change and move on with their lives? Allison has moved on and found happiness. Scott didn't ruin her life, Scott did not put her in a situation where she could be beaten routinely and left for dead in that awful prison.

Allison doesn't have to be on guard all the time because she is afraid of when the next beating will come for her, or even who it will be. The cops didn't put a bash order on her. Scott will spend most of his life behind bars, does that sound fair?' asked Meg.

'No, I don't think so, but to be honest I do not know Scott, I know you. I care about you. I want happiness and love for you. I have to be honest, this whole thing sounds insane. But when you talk about him, I see you think you are in love with him. So, congratulations,' said Charlie, holding her arms wide to hug her friend.

TWENTY-NINE

Allison arrived home from the studio to find Robert had made them dinner.

'Hey, look at you, getting around the house, you have come a long way since last year,' said Allison, moving in to kiss him.

'Yes, little steps, one by one. My physio said that I am ready to move around without the crutches around the house now.

How was your day?' Robert asked, handing her a glass of wine.

'Thank you, Robert. Something has been on my mind. I never know quite how to bring it up,' said Allison.

'What is it, Allison? You look worried, now I am worried, just tell me.' He took the seat across from her.

Ally exhaled. 'When you were in hospital, in a coma, on life support, the doctors were pushing me as your wife and next of kin to either turn off the machine and risk you not being able to support yourself. They said I needed to find an end-of-life statement. I didn't even know if you had prepared one or not. They said if you hadn't, I had to decide. Well, I couldn't, so Amber and I searched our apartment for a statement. It meant opening your will,' said Allison.

The colour drained from his face.

'We found your will, we found that you have a son that you left money to, which is not the problem, the first was and is that you had a child and did not tell me about him, the second was maybe you had an affair.' She held her hand up to stop him speaking.

'Amber did some digging. I know that you didn't have an affair while we were together, we know the boy is seventeen, and that he is your sister-in-law's son. You had an affair with your sister-in-law. I guess I know now why you and your brother didn't get along, but why didn't you tell me?'

'I am sorry, Allison, I should have told you. I meant to, if that is any consolation, and I was going to when I was home that time and then we were talking about starting our own family, and then the attack, and *pow*, here we are. I didn't have an affair with my brother's wife, she was my girlfriend first. She left me when she found out that she was expecting and tricked my brother into believing that it was his baby. She thought he had better prospects than me and would make a better husband and father material than I would, and at the time she was right. I was young, just finishing school and preparing to leave for basic training.'

'I see. When did she tell you?' asked Allison.

'She didn't, they spent a few years trying for a second baby. When they went to see specialists, it turned out that my brother has azoospermia which means that he doesn't produce sperm. She had to tell him that Joshua is not his baby. My brother then insisted on a DNA test, which showed Joshua was from the same gene pool. Of course, he blamed me, then her, and then I was told that I could never see Joshua again.'

'Wow, that must have been hard for you,' said Allison.

'Yes and no. The kid has a great family, both are doting parents. He is my son, but I am not raising him. I started putting money away when I found out because I thought if they split, or worse if anything happened to them, Joshua would need some support, for school, a car, anything. Meanwhile, I will stay out of their way and let them be happy together.'

'That is incredible. Half of your family have written you off because of what she has done. You miss out on Christmas and family events because your brother and his family are there,' said Allison.

'The truth is, Ally, I was hurt firstly by what she did and secondly because of what my brother did, in going with her so fast, knowing how I felt about her, it just wasn't right. Baby or not, then when he found out I had been doubly duped he blamed me. So, the truth is I want nothing to do with people that act that way. It is wrong, they are wrong, and I don't need that in my life, in our life. I am truly sorry that I didn't tell you. To be honest, most of the time I just put it out of my head. I just wanted to be with you, to build my life and my family with you,' said Robert.

'Thank you for telling me. I should have known you wouldn't keep a secret from me on purpose,' said Allison.

'No, it wasn't that I didn't want you to know, I really do just have a head full of us, is all,' said Robert.

The water Robert had put on the stove for pasta was boiling over. He jumped up to take it off the heat but stumbled and landed on the floor. She was at his side in a second, looking into his face. 'Are you okay?' said Allison.

'Yes.' He rolled onto his back and pulled her on top of him. They kissed, exploring each other.

The fan whirred in the corner. Allison straddled Robert, feeling him hard through his pants. She took an ice cube from her drink, held the ice against his chest, rolled it to his nipple, blew gently on the cold, licked the water running across his chest. When it melted away, she took another cube from the ice bucket and ran it the length of his shoulders, across one then along the nape of his neck to the other side. He shuddered, rubbed her thighs, lifted himself into her.

Allison's hot breath was in his ear while running the ice down his torso to his belly button. She raised herself up enough to release him from his pants, running the length of him with her hand. Squeezing firmly. Enjoying the feel of him in her hands. Without taking off her own bottoms, Allison moved the fabric of her underwear to the side and pushed him inside of her. Lowering herself onto him, she was wet and took his hardness deep inside of her.

She reached for another ice cube and tucked her hand behind herself so that the ice was resting at the base of his cock. He shuddered, the cold shocked and excited him. Robert bucked under her, and she rode him to orgasm. It was brief. She stayed on top of him to feel him go limp. Their juices flowed from her. Allison's hair spread on his chest, straining his neck to kiss her, they luxuriated on each other's lips.

'I am so happy you are mine. You are perfect,' said Robert.

'Same. I cannot remember ever feeling so relaxed, loved, and in love,' said Allison.

Allison sat up and lifted herself from him, returning his

pants back to modesty. 'Dinner should be ready soon. I should set the table.'

'Allison.' He took her hand. 'I am getting stronger all the time. I want us to start our own family. What do you think? I know it will be awkward and interfere with your career, but I was thinking, I enjoy taking care of you, and my time is nearly up in the air force. The pension they will give me is respectable, and I could work from home and take care of the babies.'

'Babies?' asked Allison.

'Well, I don't know how many you want to make, do I, and I certainly do not want to put any limits on our family,' said Robert.

'Me either, and I was doing some thinking too. I have had a lot of time to think about how I want our life to look when you woke up. I want to sing, yes, but I do not want to have to travel away from home so much. I want to be with you and our babies. I am going to finish this album it won't be my last and with help from Mark at the studio we are going to push the album more on YouTube and Spotify. He is going to help me design and find the people to build a studio, right in our very own house back in Fremantle. He is from there too and spends half his time there. Robert, I want to go home. Nothing good for us has happened here. a career is just not that important. I only ever wanted to make enough money for us to get by on. This city life is not for me, and it certainly is no place to raise our children.'

'Thank god, I am so glad that you said that. I miss our home too. What are the chances that we could buy our old house back?'

'There is only one way to find out. Let's contact the agent and have him make an offer they can't refuse,' said Allison.

THIRTY

S cott got dressed in the suit that Meg had delivered to the prison the day before. His stag-do was yoga and cake with the guys from class. A small group that had grown around him in support for his and Meg's impending nuptials.

'I really cannot believe that this is happening,' he reflected to the image of himself in the mirror.

'Me either,' came the voice of the warden behind him. 'But you don't scrub up half bad.'

'Thank you, sir,' said Scott.

'You don't deserve her, and I don't believe that you deserve a second chance on the outside either. I also don't believe that she deserves to spend what is left of her youth waiting for you, being married to a man that cannot properly be a husband to her. That said, the chaplain believes that she is good for you, that she has let out the nicer, more pleasant side of you, and that with her you are no longer a danger to society. Still, it will be a long while before I ever put you up for parole. I just don't believe that these last two years have made that much difference to the monster that was brought in here. However, I am not the one marrying you, I wouldn't, apart for the obvious I don't believe that you deserve a second chance. Meg does. She believes in you, and there is many a free man that would give his right arm for a woman to love him that way. How she loves you.'

'I know, warden, I know I don't deserve her, I know she doesn't deserve me, but she wants me, warden. She loves me, and she freely sacrifices a normal marriage on the outside to be half a wife to me on the inside. Meg may be a little tapped in the head for doing this, but love is love. She loves me. She makes my life matter when so many other people in the world are prepared to throw me away like yesterday's scraps. My Meg turns up here every week to love me. She writes me, she phones me, she lets me touch her in the family hut, she whispers in my ears that she loves me. Do you have someone so perfect loving you out there? Are you so lucky, warden? I hope so. You are not a bad man, and you deserve it,' said Scott.

'Are we ready?' asked the chaplain from the door.

'Definitely,' said Scott.

They stood in the small chapel of the prison. Efforts had been made to fit the occasion, the chaplain had put flowers around the room, a white ribbon linked the chairs and ended with a bow at the aisle, the warden and two prison guards were present as witnesses. One witness hit play on his phone, and a tinny rendition of the wedding march filled the room. All eyes turned as Meg appeared in the doorway. She wore the dress her mother wore when she married Harrison just over a year ago, white lace and silk fitted to her rounded frame. Her hair was swept up in a French style with flower sprigs for decoration. A guard took photos of her as she walked down the short aisle.

Meg took her place next to Scott.

'You look beautiful,' he said and kissed her unveiled cheek.

'I am so nervous,' she said, handing her flowers to a guard behind her. The guard smiled. It could have been any other wedding that he had seen on the outside, except that this was between Scott Clarke and a prison yoga teacher.

They exchanged their vows as any couple would do. He gave her a ring, his mother's ring, sent to him when she died. He thought it was such a stupid thing to leave him, but now he understood. She had hoped for him to find peace. As any mother would for their son. Now it would be forever carried on the finger of the woman that he loved.

He recited a poem that he wrote for the occasion.

The chaplain pronounced them as man and wife. He kissed his bride. The small crowd cheered and threw confetti. Meg laughed as they posed for photos, signed the marriage certificate, and thanked the chaplain.

'I can't believe that we are married,' said Meg.

'I can't believe you went through with it. I am so happy right now my chest is ripe for bursting,' said Scott.

'Congratulations,' said the warden, shaking Scott's hand and kissing the bride on the cheek.

'Thank you, warden, for everything,' said Scott.

'Well, as you know, I have my reservations, but you are right. For some ungodly reason, this girl loves you, and you love her. I have arranged for you both to have a short honeymoon in the family suite. Lunch has been prepared, and you have the room until six, at which time I am afraid that Mrs Clarke will be accompanied to her car and Mr Clarke back to his cell.'

'Yes, of course, warden, thank you for everything that you have done for us today,' said Meg.

'Anything in the name of rehabilitation and true love, Mrs Clarke.'

They had decorated the family suite like a hotel room, except everything movable was bolted down to a secured surface.

'You wouldn't believe how nervous I feel,' said Meg.

The chef had set out a meal of chicken and salad with baked potatoes, accompanied by a bottle of non-alcoholic apple cider.

'This is really nice. Are all your meals like this?' asked Meg.

'I wish. This is amazing and certainly above and beyond the usual fare.' Under a serviette in the centre of the table there were two cupcakes decorated with flowers.

'This really is wonderful. I don't think I have ever felt this happy,' said Meg.

'You deserve so much more than this, and I will give the world when I can. I am going to try and get out of here as soon as they can. I am going to be the best prisoner in all the world's correction centres so I can get out and make a life with you.'

'That will be wonderful, and now we can make our plans here,' said Meg. She stood up and took his hand as he stood up in front of her.

'You look beautiful, so beautiful,' said Scott. Taking her face in the palms of his hands, he kissed her. Softly, testing his way, teasing her with his tongue. 'Heavenly. I truly don't deserve you,' said Scott.

'Please shut up and take me to bed,' said Meg.

'Wait, let me watch you undress.' He moved towards her and cupped her face in his hands, kissing her deeply.

She pulled him towards the bed. Scott helped her slide her camisole over her head. He explored her body softly with kisses, returning to her mouth gently. Hungry for him, she answered by kissing him deeper. She groaned as he kissed her neck and then moved down to the valley of her breasts. Meg arched her back, giving herself to him. He eagerly took one breast, then the other, into his mouth. He nibbled and teased her with his tongue, moving from one breast then the other.

Meg was wet, she wanted him deep inside of her. Her pulse quickened as one of his hands moved lower into her panties. Rubbing along the sleek wetness of her desire, he found her entrance and pushed one, then two fingers deep inside to explore her. Her back arched to meet his hand. He kissed her soft lips while his fingers instinctively brought her to climax. Her tight muscles clamped down around his fingers, and he wanted to be inside her.

Meg lowered her panties. Scott took the cue and removed his own revealing his hardness. Meg kicked her panties off as she wrapped a hand around the width of him, feeling him become even harder. She gently squeezed the silky-soft, hard texture of him. She pulled him gently as he positioned himself above her. Meg guided him into her folds. Wet slickness clamped around him, squeezing him as he pushed slowly inside her.

Their eyes locked. Scott was struggling to constrain himself. He slowed down to follow Meg's lead. Each time Meg pushed back at him, he pumped a little harder. He kissed her mouth, her neck, and made his way back to her right nipple. He took the pink rosebud into his mouth, grazed it with his teeth, teased it harder with his tongue.

Meg's hands were stretched above her head, gripping the bars of the bedhead. She surrendered to her body, to the pleasure he was giving her.

They responded quicker to each other. Blood raced,

pumped. An orgasm took over every inch of Meg's body. She shuddered as she held onto him. Felt him explode inside her. 'Oh my god,' gasped Scott before his head collapsed into the nook of her neck.

Scott lay down next to Meg. She turned on her side away from him so that she nestled her back against his torso. Spent, he snuggled up behind her, one arm around her body. He pulled her into him and held her until the bell sounded the warning that their time together was nearly over.

'I really don't want to go,' said Meg.

'Of course, you don't. I don't want you to go either, but we have to be ready when the guard comes. We cannot lose our visiting privileges, I could not go on if I couldn't see you,' said Scott.

'Would they do that?' asked Meg.

'Yes, there are many rules and regulations that we must follow inside here and outside too. We were very lucky today that the warden is such a sad sack romantic that we had this long in here,' said Scott.

'Okay, I understand, and, yes, it is sad and annoying, but it is worth it to be here with you. I will dream about you until the next time. And then the next.'

'I will relive every second of today. The way you walked down the aisle, your smile, and, oh, your kiss, the way your body feels. I have to stop talking, we should get dressed and tidy up the room. We have to unmake the bed and dump it all in the laundry chute.'

'Easily done, and worth it for what we have just shared, Mr Clarke.'

'Well, I am glad you found everything to your satisfaction, Mrs Clarke.'

'Oh, it definitely is. Please make sure that you do everything in your power to ensure that we get to do this again soon, my love,' said Meg.

'Every month is the schedule, all being well. I will think about you every day. I guess we are lucky in that you live close by and come in weekly to teach yoga too. You will be okay, won't you, Meg?' asked Scott.

'Okay, how?'

'With this version of a marriage, never knowing what is going to happen from one visit to the next and how long it will be before we can be together again,' said Scott.

'Yes. My only friend that knows, Charlie, thought I was nuts. She thinks it is a crazy thing to do, until I explained to her that she didn't know you, she doesn't know you how I know you, that you are not the same man with me, the same man you were before when you met Allison and did those things they write about whenever your name is mentioned. People don't give you a chance, do they?'

'In here, yes and no. I am not the worst criminal here, and sometimes people like the warden or the doctor see me as still a man, a person, human, and treat me with a dignity that makes me feel whole and normal, or as close to normal as I can be. Then there is you, Meg. You make me sing every single day. For you I want to be good, I want to be a good man. I will show you when I get out of here just how good you have made me. You have made me a better man, and one day I will spend the rest of life proving it to you. Meg, don't cry, I will see you on Friday in yoga. And I will write to you tomorrow. You can call Thursday and come and visit me on the weekend.'

The warden walked Scott back to his cell. There were cheers and jeers from the men as he paraded down the corridor to his cell. He lay on his bunk and thought about Meg. She would be in her car now, driving out of the gate. He knew she was thinking about him because that was the kind of girl she was, thoughtful and kind, and yes, the warden was right, much too good for him.

He had dinner with some men from his yoga group that he had become friends with over the last year. He told them about the ceremony, the lunch, and the extra time they got to have in the family suite. They congratulated him and wished they had half of his luck.

Scott wanted to be alone with his thoughts, so he skipped recreation time in the common room and retired to his cell. There was a movie special showing tonight, so the halls and other cells were empty. He rolled out his yoga mat and waited for the sound of Meg's voice to come. He followed her instructions to slow his breathing, reach his arms for Father Sky and surrendered down, reaching his hands to Mother Earth. Together the creator of all things.

Scott didn't hear them coming because Meg's voice had filled his ears. He felt his legs taken out from under him, his face held down with someone's shoe, pressing it into his yoga mat. He spoke her name without making a sound as the group of henchmen bludgeoned his arms, legs, and body. The leader struck the killer blow to his crown. 'That's for taking my time slot in the shag suite. You are too good for her. I make sure that she knows it was me that did her this favour.'

Scott's world turned to blackness. In the dark, he bled out alone but for Meg's voice calling him home.

When the guards found his body, they used his own blanket to cover his body and carry him through the prison to the infirmary. By the time the warden arrived, the mess in his room had been cleaned, and his personal items, the ones that were not of any use to the other inmates, were boxed up and waiting for collection with his body.

The warden approved a prison burial for Scott to save Meg the expense of a funeral. There was no one on the outside that gave a shit about this man, no one except her, and he would like to save her the trouble. He took the box of Scott Clarkes belongings and left the prison.

He drove the short distance to Meg's house and waited at her door before ringing the bell. She was singing, and he was tempted to leave her the box and call her in the morning, take the chicken shit's way out. 'No,' he told himself, 'I owe her more than that.'

When he rang the bell, Meg swung it open. A large rotti trapped between her legs eyed him cautiously.

'Warden, this is a surprise, is something wrong? Would you like to come in?' asked Meg.

'Yes, please.' He followed her into the house, and Ralph followed him. The warden took the seat she offered him in the lounge room.

'I am afraid I have some terrible news. Tonight, just before lock up they found Scott's body in his cell. They had jumped him. We think that there were a few of them, and, well, they got the better of him. There was a movie playing in the recreation room, so most of the men were in there. I am sorry. I don't really know what else to say. I have arranged for a service at the prison. It won't cost you anything that way, and I have been told that you can have the marriage annulled. It is up to you,' said the Warden.

'Dead, dead,' repeated Meg.

'Yes, I am sorry,' said the warden. 'Can I get you a drink? A cup of tea? Call someone for you?'

'What is that?' Meg nodded towards the box he was holding.

'This is his personal things from his cell. They belong to you now, as you are his next of kin, his wife.'

'Yes, I am his wife, and I intend for it to stay that way. I am not ashamed to be the wife of Scott Clarke.'

'No, you shouldn't be. He really turned around in the last couple of years; I thought you were both going to make it,' said the warden.

'But we didn't. We didn't stand a chance. You didn't protect him, you couldn't, those men run all over you, and you let them for a bit of peace. Who are the men that killed my husband? As his wife, I am entitled to answers,' said Meg.

'Yes, you are, and we are doing everything to find out who it was. They will be brought to justice. I promise you.'

'Thank you, warden. I don't suppose that there is anything else you can do. You can't bring him back to me. I must have had the shortest marriage in history. I will be okay, I will cry myself to sleep and won't be in to work this week or next week. Maybe not at all. I will let you know. Thank you for coming by to tell me personally, it means something.'

'Like I said, it is the least I can do,' said the warden as he let himself out of Meg's house.

Meg listened to the sound of the warden driving away before getting herself up to pour herself another glass of wine. Her wedding dress and flowers from the day lay across her kitchen table. She twirled the ring around her finger, thought of the promise he made her that she was sure he would have followed through on.

It was over as fast as it had begun. Fifteen minutes earlier she was a happily married woman to a man spending life in prison, with a slim chance of early parole. But he was getting better all the time, he was getting stronger all the time, soon those prison bullies would not have been able to beat on him, use him as a punching bag and treat him like a victim. One day he could have turned around and pummelled them right back and even made them eat the soap.

DON'T MISS OUT!

Visit the website below and you can sign up to receive emails whenever Vanessa McKay publishes a new book. There's no charge and no obligation.
https://books2read.com/r/B-A-ATSJ-ISRBC

Connecting independent readers to independent writers.

Did you love *When Loves Heals the Heart?*
Then you should read *Allison* by Vanessa McKay!

Allison's life is about to change forever. At twenty-five she is alone and free to make her own decisions. Allison is determined to follow her dreams to become a singer and a woman in charge of her own destiny.

Scott Clarke is a serial killer in the making with his sights fixed firmly on Allison. Scott threatens to turn Allison's dreams into nightmares.

One by one he eliminates those closest to her.

Can Allison escape him to live the life she dreams of with her new beau Robert?

Read more at Vanessa McKay's site.

ABOUT THE AUTHOR

Vanessa McKay is a Western Australian author of women's fiction whose stories explore the tender, complicated terrain of love, loss, and the courage it takes to begin again.

Love Heals the Heart is her latest novel, continuing the story of characters readers have followed across her fiction — including Allison, the tragic yet triumphant heroine who first captured hearts in Vanessa's debut novel of the same name.

Her debut, Allison, introduced readers to a woman navigating profound hardship with quiet resilience — a story of darkness, survival, and ultimately, hope. Bali Retreat swept readers to sun-drenched Balinese landscapes where love and second chances collide, and When Lucy Came Down from the Ferris Wheel showcased her gift for capturing the small, luminous moments that quietly change everything.

When she's not writing fiction, Vanessa facilitates creative writing retreats for women across Australia and Bali, helping others find their voice and their stories. She believes deeply that women's stories matter — and that it's never too late to tell them.

She lives in Western Australia with her family.

www.ingramcontent.com/pod-product-compliance
Lightning Source LLC
Chambersburg PA
CBHW061102100726
47911CB00012B/355